Breakwater Skeleton Unknown

The Cherrystone Creek Mysteries: Book II

Emma Jackson

All Rights Reserved. Copyright © 2020
Smith Beach Press

This is a work of fiction. Any resemblance to actual persons, living or dead, are purely happenstance. The names used in the book are composites of names common to the area, to assure verisimilitude. All rights reserved, including the right to reproduce this book, or portions thereof, in any form. No part of this text may be reproduced, transmitted, downloaded, decompiled, reverse engineered, or stored in or introduced into any information storage and retrieval system, in any form or by any means, whether electronic or mechanical without the express written permission of the author. The scanning, uploading, and distribution of this book via the Internet or via any other means without the permission of the author is illegal and punishable by law. Please purchase only authorized electronic editions, and do not participate in or encourage electronic piracy of copyrighted materials.

Editing by Debbie Maxwell Allen
Cover by Shayne Rutherford
Dark Moon Graphics

Interior Design by Colleen Sheehan
Ampersand Book Designs
Back Cover and Amazon Blurbs by Shelley Ring

SMITHBEACHPRESS.COM

Ebook ISBN-13: 978-1-7338928-6-5
Paperback ISBN-13: 978-1-7338928-7-2

Prologue

THE COAST GUARD Boatswain Mate Art Davis set a security zone around the four southernmost World War II concrete liberty ships sunk as a breakwater offshore at Kiptopeke State Park. He'd been here all night and now was watching the sky lightening into the rose and orange of sunrise.

As the sun rose from the east it set The Bay side of the ships into sharp shadowed relief making them almost pretty. Davis knew from experience they weren't pretty. They were in fact stained, cracked, and crumbling concrete. They were good for the wildlife both above and below the water, but they were dangerous hulks for anyone venturing too close.

As a seaman it hurt Boatswain Davis to see these old ships slowly yielding to the punishing effects of the weather and The Bay. "What a way to go," he murmured to himself.

Breakwater Skeleton Unknown

It was the end ship, the S.S. Edwin Thacher, that the night before was the point of impact for the speeding yellow Cigarette boat, racing to avoid arrest. At roughly eighty knots the fast boat — essentially two huge engines with a composite shell around them—running headlong into a solidly grounded massive concrete ship ... well, the concrete wins.

The boat ended up in little pieces, difficult to recover, as did the driver of the boat, who was attempting to flee before being arrested, his flight cut short by the Thacher.

Once the security zone was in place, commercial salvors went to work carefully recovering whatever they could. The two Mercury 565 horsepower racing engines were lifted from the sandy bottom by a barge-mounted crane. The inertia created by the engines contributed greatly to the total destruction when the speeding boat hit the ship. As the forward motion of the boat suddenly stopped they were ripped from their mounts and kept racing forward. Pressurized gasoline from the 224-gallon fuel tanks aerosolized creating a fine cloud of gasoline and air—phenomenally explosive. As the deep cycle marine batteries tore loose their cables sparked setting off the air-gasoline mixture. The explosion was glorious. As they flew forward the engines crushed everything and everyone in the cockpit before pancaking bits of the hull and the driver between themselves and the concrete, then falling to the seabed.

The demolition was so complete that other than the engines the salvors were only able to recover some small practically unidentifiable bits and pieces of metal, like the anchor and its rode, and little else. Virtually nothing organic remained, and what hadn't been literally vaporized in the collision and explosion had been gathered up for breakfast by the bottom-feeding fish and crabs populating the breakwater environs.

While the salvage crew worked, Davis' crewmen, Seamen Dixon and Buckles, decided on an adventure—they'd explore the concrete hulk. This was normally forbidden as the deterioration was severe and the risks of injury high, but that never deterred kids, and that's what these teen-aged seamen were.

They had Bos'n Davis ease the RHIB (Rigid Hull Inflatable Boat) in close to one of the breaks in the side of the Thacher, where they'd be able to pull themselves up and over the rail. Donning heavy gloves to keep from shredding their hands on the rusty steel and concrete they pulled themselves aboard.

SN Buckles pulled himself over the rail, landing on his feet. But his feet seemed to settle into something soft.

He looked down. The deck was thickly covered in aromatic seabird guano, at least four inches deep. He heard Dixon scrabbling at the rusted rail behind him. He thought about warning him, but as he started to turn Dixon vaulted over the rail.

"What the—?" Dixon hollered, wind milling his arms. His feet started to slip, and despite his efforts he overbalanced and went down. Hard.

At the same moment the wind paused, and Buckles got a whiff of the ship without a modifying brisk breeze. He gagged. "What the heck?" He coughed against the stench. He'd wanted to laugh at Dixon's less-than-graceful landing, but the smell was making his eyes water.

He took pity on his crewmate and offered him a gloved hand up.

"You said this was going to be an adventure," sputtered a guano-seated Dixon. "This sucks. I'm going back to the boat."

"Oh come on, sissy," chided Buckles. "The breeze is coming back up so it won't be too bad. You're sure not going to do it when the sun is high and baking everything. Let's go now, walk to the bow and back, and see what we might find. Okay?"

As they made their way forward on the ship they were suddenly brought up short. There, partially hidden under some superstructure, they saw a bone. Normally that would not have been remarkable. The ship was used by pelicans, gulls, and even osprey so this might well have been left from some of their prey. Except for the size. The bone looked too large to be from a fish. Maybe it was from an animal brought here to be eaten by a bald eagle, but even that seemed unlikely. Admittedly eagles were scavengers and had been known to feed off the found carcass of a whitetail deer, but that didn't seem right.

Even though they were wearing their work uniforms they didn't want to kneel in the guano just to be able to get a better look. Hunkering down they duck-walked closer to the overhanging superstructure to see what they had found. When they saw the empty eyes of a human skull looking back at them they both started backward so precipitously that they both ended up sitting on the deck amidst the droppings.

Scrambling to their feet they rushed back to the rail and waved for the coxswain to bring the boat to pick them up.

"What happened?" asked Bos'nDavis, as he maneuvered the boat in close enough for them to jump aboard. He could see that in spite of their tans, they were both as pale as ghosts.

"Just get over here and get us off this wreck," was the reply. "We just found a body."

Chapter One

PAIGE REESE WAS trying to think clearly but she was flustered. She was at the Mallard Cove Restaurant, and sitting across the table from her was a gorgeous blue-eyed man, Special Agent Tim Hannegan of the Federal Bureau of Investigation. He was smiling at her in a most enticing manner, and she was certain that he must be able to see the color rising on her neck and infusing her cheeks. She'd called Hannegan and invited him over to the Eastern Shore just a week after she helped tie up the case of the little girl unknown. Paige was the undertaker in the county seat of Eastville. She had sought the assistance of the FBI recently and that was how she became acquainted with, and girlishly enamored of, Tim Hannegan, whom her friend Pam, the postmistress, called *Special Agent Dish*.

"Paige, I'm so happy that you called and invited me to dinner over here on The Shore. Even coming from Virginia Beach this is some of the best seafood that I have ever eaten."

"It is fresh off the charter boats," said Paige pointing out the window to the row of charter fishing boats moored stern-to at the floating docks. "When they have too good a day, the fishermen will sell their overage to the restaurant. Helps them pay for their charter, and helps the kitchen get fish so fresh they're almost still flopping."

Tim laughed as he looked around. "This place looks pretty new. Have they been in business long?"

"Well," replied Paige, picking at her crab imperial, "the marina itself has been here for ages, but it's only been a year or so since it was bought and refurbished. The restaurant was closed for quite a while and the docks were in rough shape, but some investors who own Bayside Estates and Club up the road in Accomack County bought it and have brought it back to life. They even brought the head of their culinary division, Carlos Ramirez, down to design the bar and restaurant facilities and set up the menu."

"He's done a fantastic job." Tim picked up his fork to spear one of the fire-roasted oysters and dip it in the fierySrircha lime sauce.

Paige glanced at him under her eyelashes, admiring the flex of his shoulders. "This and The Jackspot over on The Bay are about the only nighttime places down here." She rested the end of her fork on her lips in thought.

"After supper let's go over there to watch the sunset at their beach bar," said Paige. It's almost as popular as Mallory Square in Key West, although not nearly as commercial, crazy and crowded."

"That sounds like fun," said Hannegan.

After dinner they arose to head to the parking lot. When Tim took her arm to help her to the car Paige felt as though she had been tased. An electric quiver ran through her from where he was touching her elbow and settled warmly in her nether regions. She wondered if he had any similar sort of reaction.

In Paige's eyes, Special Agent Tim Hannegan was beautiful. He was just over six-feet tall and slender with almost black hair turning just a little gray at the temples. He was probably in his late thirties, and a quick habitual glance showed her no wedding ring nor suntan band where one had been. And his eyes. His eyes were just about the bluest turquoise that Paige had ever seen, and when he smiled at her, she fell deeply into them.

At The Jackspot the weather was mild so they decided to sit under the sky on the wooden patio built over the sand. Paige liked the occasional sweet drink so she ordered one of The Jackspot's specialties, the Sunset Peach with peach vodka, peach rum, peach schnapps, sour mix and cranberry juice. Looking at the ingredients made Tim's mouth pucker so he ordered a draft of Cape Charles Brewing's Cobb Island India Pale Ale.

The tide was near the ebb so there were several boats anchored at the sandbar in front of The Jackspot as the partiers awaited the sunset. Unfortunately several of the boats played loud music, their occupants gyrating to the beat either on the boat or on the sandbar. Paige thought it rather spoiled the overall atmosphere, but Hannegan didn't seem bothered.

They sat, sipping their drinks, as the sun slowly lowered and the sky took on hues of pink and blue and orangey-red.

The large billowing clouds overhead picked up the hues and seemed to glow incandescently. As the sun touched the watery horizon it seemed to melt and spread out, flattening upon the waters of The Bay. Then the orb slid silently below the horizon of the western shore and another day was closed.

On the boats on the sandbar, the besotted boaters cheered the sun's performance and poured themselves another drink in self-congratulatory celebration as if without them it never could have happened. Ignoring the drunken revelry Hannegan reached over and took Paige's hand in his. "That was beautiful," he said.

Swallowing hard Paige was only just able to croak out, "Uh huh."

"We don't get to see those over in Virginia Beach. I'll sometimes get up early enough to run on the beach and catch a sunrise, but this was special."

Hannegan turned his body to face Paige. "Watching it with you was special, too."

Hannegan's enchanting eyes drew her in. She felt that he was looking into her soul. Maintaining the eye lock Paige slowly leaned toward Hannegan. As their faces drew closer together her gaze slid from his eyes to his lips. *Oh, my goodness,* she thought, *I'm drowning.* She leaned in, closed her eyes and … her cell phone rang and vibrated loudly on the tabletop, startling both of them and destroying the moment.

"Shit," exclaimed Paige. "Oh, I'm sorry. I didn't mean to say that."

Hannegan looked amused. "Are you going to answer it?"

"Oh! Yeah!" She keyed the screen. "Hello?" she barked.

On the other end of the line was Maddie, the Northampton County Sheriff's dispatcher. "Miss Reese?"

"Yeah?" she replied in a surly voice.

"Ma'am," said the dispatcher. "I'm afraid we have a body."

This time Paige only thought the expletive but didn't say it out loud.

As the main undertaker in the county Paige also operated as the county coroner on an *ad hoc* basis, and part of the Sheriff's protocol was for her to be notified whenever there was a suspicious death.

"What's the story?"

"Well, the Coast Guard was out on one of the concrete ships at Kiptopeke, you know, cleaning up after the wreck? Well, on board the ship they found a body."

"On the ship?"

"Yes, ma'am."

"Was it fresh?"

"Ma'am?" asked the dispatcher confusedly.

"The body. Did the death seem recent?" She looked across at Hannegan shrugging her shoulders apologetically.

"Recent? No, ma'am. It's just a skeleton is all. They tagged and bagged it and are headed for your shop."

"Oh, for Pete's sake," she huffed. "Did anyone take pictures of the body *in situ?*"

"In what, ma'am?" asked Maddie.

"Never mind. The Coast Guard's bringing the body?"

"No, ma'am. They passed it over to Deputy Holland, and he's got it in the trunk of his patrol car."

Paige realized that the Eastern Shore was not Philadelphia, but she realized that she was going to have to do some crime scene protection training for the local law enforcement. For her own sake, if nothing else.

"Okay, I'm down at The Jackspot. I'll head to my office right now. Tell Holland to wait for me at the funeral home … or else he's going to have that skeleton rattling around in his trunk all night long." She hung up the phone.

"Well, crap," she said to Hannegan.

He looked at her. "Hey, requirements of the job. We'll do this again soon. Don't you worry.

"Come on," he said. "I'll drive you up to Eastville."

Paige was glad that it was dark in the car as they drove up the highway. She was sure that her massive disappointment was plain on her face, and she didn't want him to notice. Truth be told she was almost in tears.

Back in Eastville, Hannegan left the motor running as he walked Paige to the door. "Paige, I really enjoyed this evening. In spite of its precipitous ending."

Paige half laughed. "Yeah, me too, Tim. Please, let's do it again soon." She leaned into him hoping for a goodnight kiss, and was disappointed when he pressed his lips to her cheek before bouncing down the steps and walking back to his car.

Paige turned back to the front door, which was not locked, and went in to wait for Deputy Holland and his package of bones.

Chapter Two

AS SHE WAITED for the body, well, the skeleton, to be delivered Paige thought about where it had been found. The ship was one of nine World War II concrete liberty ships that had been grounded as a breakwater to protect the wharf where the cross-Bay ferry used to dock. The ferry had departed when the Chesapeake Bay Bridge-Tunnel had opened in 1974, and the ships left to slowly disintegrate under the punishment of The Bay and the weather. The ferry landing site was now a state park, and Paige had picnicked there when she was younger. She remembered watching a pair of osprey that nested in one of the wrecks, and how the seagulls (her father referred to them as flying rats because of their propensity to eat garbage) used to hover and dive and perch on the ships. Paige had always thought that they were probably eating leftover bits of fish from osprey meals. Now she wondered if they had been feasting on human bodies then, too. The thought made her shiver, and she forcibly pushed it away.

The evening was pleasant so Paige had opened the windows and turned off the air conditioning in most of the building. She could smell the sweet aroma of the climbing roses that entwined the columns on the front porch of the home, and hear the symphony of cicadas. It also allowed her to hear the crunch of gravel when the patrol car carrying the body drove around to the back of the facility.

Her workroom was windowless and the air conditioning was always on. Paige shivered as she walked through. *At least this one won't have to go into the cooler, if he's really just a skeleton*, she thought.

She snatched open the back door just as Deputy Holland had his fist raised to knock.

"Oh, my gosh, Paige," he blurted. "You scared the heck out of me. Bad enough driving around with this skeleton in my trunk. I can't tell you what tricks my imagination has been playing on me, and then you startle me with the door!"

Chris Holland was very young and very new in the Sheriff's Department. He wore his uniform with obvious pride and had an unfortunate tendency to walk with a bit of a swagger. He had been hired after the previous senior deputy had died in an accident while racing his Cigarette boat away from the law. His pride was at stake at the moment.

Paige laughed, "Sorry. Didn't mean to … spook you."

"Very funny. Very clever. C'mon, help me get this guy out of my trunk."

"If it's really just a skeleton it can't weigh more than about twenty-five pounds. You can't handle it?"

"C'mon, Paige. It's the skeleton and his clothes and the body bag … and it's just awkward, all right? C'mon. Give me a hand."

Paige wheeled a gurney out to the patrol car as the deputy popped the trunk. "I want him treated just like a deceased body, with dignity" she said.

"Well, down to Kiptopeke they just sort of tossed the bag into my trunk."

Paige's gut started a slow boil. "They may have down there, but here I'm in charge, and the deceased will be treated with the courtesy and respect he's due."

"Yes, ma'am," he muttered, thinking, *heck, it's just a pile of old bones, not the Pope.*

The rubberized body bag had strap handles on all four sides. Paige took one end and the deputy the other, and they lifted the bag out of the car trunk and onto the gurney. There wasn't much weight or fullness to it.

"You need help gettin' it inside?"

"No, deputy, you've done fine. Go on. Get your car blessed or exorcised or whatever you want to do."

Nodding at Paige, the deputy climbed into his car and hastened away. She laughed quietly. Lots of people just couldn't cope with dead bodies. Paige knew they were just empty receptacles, the person and the life essence gone. She also knew, though, that lots of people were superstitious, whether they admitted it or not ... even to themselves.

She wheeled the gurney back inside and locked the door behind her. It was getting late, but she was curious. She wanted to see what had been dropped in her lap. Pulling on a white Tyvek suit, Nitrile gloves and a Honeywell Particulate Disposable Mask she unzipped the body bag.

As she had feared the skeleton inside was all jumbled together and mixed with the scraps of clothing that remained. What she hadn't counted on was the coating of guano that covered everything and stuck bird feathers to some of the bones. There was even a bird's nest in the ribcage. The rubber boots had just been tossed in, and as the body bag had been shifted around they acted as mixing paddles to stir everything together. She wheeled the gurney next to a stainless-steel work table and started removing each bone.

First she gently removed the scraps of clothing, checking each to ensure that there were no bone fragments or other evidence tangled up in them. The clothes she set off to the side, at the very end of the work table, and then she was left with a body bag of bones.

Paige was grateful for the anatomy classes she had taken while studying for her mortician's certificate as she gently removed each bone from the body bag. She tried to place each bone in its correct place on the table. It was like doing a macabre jigsaw puzzle.

Let's see. Scapula back here. Wait, is that the left or the right one? Hmmm. Okay, the pubic arc and the narrow iliac crest mean that this is definitely a man, not a woman. This must be the ulna. That's lucky—the patella is still attached to the femur by ligaments, and this is the shin for the same leg. "Oh the knee bone connected to the shin bone, and the shin bone connected to the ankle bone, and the ankle bone connected to the foot bone, oh hear the Word of the Lord." *Darn. An ear worm. That song is going to be running through my mind as long as I have to work on this body ... uh, skeleton.*

Paige walked over and turned on her radio. *Maybe WESR can keep that song from driving me crazy,* she thought.

Paige turned the body bag inside out to make sure she had found everything the Coast Guardsmen had haphazardly thrown in. Then she returned to her body puzzle.

She started examining each individual bone more closely searching for any anomalies. She still talked to herself as she worked. *Okay, let's see, this second phalange on the right foot is crooked. Looks like it was broken but not set. 'Course, mostly you just tape a broken toe to the next toe to it. There's a healed break on the right fibula, but it looks pretty old, too. Wonder if he broke them at the same time?*

This femur looks kind of fresh. I wonder how long it takes for a bone exposed to the elements to become bleached and brittle. Bet I can't find that out on Google.

Paige continued examining the bones looking for something, anything, that might give her a hint about how this guy had died.

Oh, wait. The hyoid bone. It's totally crushed. I know what caused that. This guy was most probably strangled.

Finding a probable cause of death didn't help Paige figure out an identity, though. She had his mandibles, so when she got closer to an identity she'd hopefully be able to verify it with dental records, but that was only if they could find a probable locality so she could narrow down to a workable number of dentists. If he was from The Shore that would be a lot easier than if she had to go over to the Norfolk area. *If I have to go to the western shore maybe Tim can use his FBI contacts to help me out.*

Paige glanced at the clock hanging over the door. Two a.m. She had been working on the skeleton for hours. She yawned hugely. *I've got to get some sleep. I'll get back to this guy in the morning.*

Rather than driving back out to her apartment at Wilkins Beach Paige climbed the steps to the apartment her daddy used to live in on the top floor of the funeral home. She had left it the way it was when Daddy was still alive, though she had let Nott live there while they worked out his legal problems after he found the body of the little girl unknown. He had since returned to his hermitic life in the oyster house in Cherrystone Creek.

Chapter Three

WHEN THE CLOCK radio woke Paige she had only slept for three hours. She was muzzy-headed and wasn't sure if she had heard the radio correctly. *A hurricane? That's all we need.*

She hurried into the kitchen and while the Keurig warmed up she turned the little television on the counter to WAVY-10 news from Norfolk. Sure enough, a hurricane that had been messing around in northern Florida for several days had suddenly seemed to make up its mind and was now making a beeline for the Chesapeake Bay.

Oh, that's just wonderful, thought Paige. *As if I didn't have enough on my plate already. A hurricane. Named Darrell, of all things.*

Paige dressed, went out to Machipongo Trading Company for a cafe con leche to go, and drove back of the old County Courthouse to the Sheriff's department. As she entered the dispatcher, Maddie, looked up. "Howdy, Miss Paige. You ready for the storm?"

Ignoring the question Paige asked, "Who's working on the dead body at Kiptopeke case?"

Maddie just looked at her. "Kiptopeke case? Oh, you mean that skeleton the Coast Guardsmen found on the old ship? I suppose that's the Coast Guard's case, isn't it?"

With her lack of sleep and no breakfast pastry Paige was short-tempered. "No, the Coast Guard shouldn't be investigating it. It's not a 'death at sea.' It's just a dead body, or skeleton, their people happened to find. It's not their jurisdiction."

"Well, ma'am, I'm not sure …"

"Is the sheriff here? Or the county attorney?" Paige was escalating things, but that's what need to happen.

"Now, Miss Paige, you don't need to go bothering them. You wait here. I'll see if Deputy Holland knows anything."

Chris Holland, looking sharp in his crisp deputy's uniform, came out from the back. "Hey, Paige," he said. "You here about that skeleton?"

Paige nodded and he led her into a small conference room off to the side. She'd been in the room before, but it still depressed her. There were no windows and the walls were painted an institutional bilious green. If you weren't nauseous when you entered the room, you soon would be between the color scheme and the odor of strong disinfectant.

"Chris, did you or any crime scene people go over where the body was found?"

"I don't think so, Paige. The Coast Guardsmen found it. I don't know if they had CGIS come over from Norfolk, but I sure doubt it." He looked around as if checking for eavesdroppers and lowered his voice. "Believe it or not the Coasties found it while they were scooping up the pieces from Pablo's ... you know ... accident."

"Accident?" laughed Paige. "Doesn't 'accident' indicate something that happened ... well, accidently? He was running from the law. I don't think that qualifies as an 'accident'."

Holland swallowed loudly in embarrassment.

"How are you handling the new promotion since Senior Deputy Pablo's untimely demise?"

"Uh ... well ..." stammered Holland.

"Right," said Paige. "Again, did any of your people work the scene?"

"Well how about your people?"

"Our people? Who? The Coast Guardsmen took some pictures with their phones, but no one from our department went out. The Coast Guardsmen said they brought everything that was there. Wasn't nobody here wanted to go out there. You know how nasty those old ships are with bird poop?" He made a comical face.

"So no one at all searched the actual crime scene?"

Holland scratched his head. "Well, Paige, now that wasn't really the crime scene. I mean, that's not where the murder took place."

"You're sure of that?" Paige asked.

"Well ... I guess. I mean, there's no sign of it."

"Chris, there was no sign that there was a body there in the first place. And it was there so long that it became a skeleton. For Pete's sake, we don't know where he was killed, how long the body was there, or anything. Did anyone search for a weapon?"

"No, I guess not. Well, I'll tell you this—I ain't going out there. Especially with that hurricane coming."

"Somebody better get out there quick. Especially with that hurricane coming."

"Have fun, Paige," said Chris. He unfolded is tall frame and left the conference room.

Paige went back to her office at the funeral home. She was going to have to do it herself. Of course. *Why doesn't anyone else have any initiative,* she wondered to herself?

One thing Paige knew for certain was that she wasn't going out to the ship alone. She'd have to get Nott to go with her. He helped out on her last adventure. She was sure he'd be up for helping her again.

JAMES NOTTINGHAM SMITH, Nott for short, was a disabled Army veteran. He was coping well with the physical limitations he suffered when an IED in Fallujah blew him up, but his PTSD, though presently controlled, could quickly tip him into an almost catatonic state. Working with Paige had helped him get a handle on reality.

Nott lived in a deserted Oyster Guard House standing on stilts in Cherrystone Creek near Cape Charles. The house had no amenities at all, so Paige couldn't call him. He had even refused a cell phone, so Paige was going to have to send someone in a boat.

Back in her office Paige called her friend DonnaBozza, the Executive Director of the Citizens for a Better Eastern Shore, to ask for her husband's help. "Donna, this is Paige. Do you think Jim could run up Cherrystone to Nott's shack and tell him that I need his help?"

"What's going on, Paige?" she asked.

"You heard about the skeleton they found on the old ship at the ferry landing? I've got him here in my workroom. The sheriff's looking into it, but I'm afraid they aren't going to go into enough depth."

Paige imagined Donna nibbling on her Bic pen as she sat at her desk in the old home that housed the Citizens for a Better Eastern Shore near the courthouse. "Paige, you know Sheriff Grainger doesn't want you messing with his cases anymore."

"Donna, I know. But as coroner I have the right and the responsibility to do certain investigations."

"Paige, you're not the coroner."

"Well, *ad hoc* coroner. It does give me some responsibilities and some authority. You know that, Donna. Heck, without me and Nott they never would have found out about those little girls that went missing."

"Yeah, I know, but –"

"I'm not going to do anything stupid," Paige interrupted. "Or dangerous. Or illegal. I just want ... well, I want to go out to that ship and look around. Doesn't seem like anyone else has done crime scene investigation. And, Donna, that is well within the purview of the coroner."

Donna's deep sigh came clearly across the phone. "Okay. I'll call Jim and see if he can run out to Nott's."

"Oh, thank you so much, Donna. And once Nott and I have hooked up do you think Jim could run us out to the ship, too?"

Again a deep sigh. "Okay, Paige. But I don't want Jim climbing up on that thing. It isn't safe. I know I don't have any sway over what you do, but he's my husband. I do have say over what he does, and I am not going to allow him to get up there with you. Okay?"

"Of course, Donna. I'd never presume to ask."

"Yeah, right," Donna said sarcastically. "Just you and Nott be real careful, too. I don't want Jim having to get up there to help you out of trouble."

"Promise, Donna. We'll be careful. We don't want to go exploring, I just have to see the location where the skeleton was."

IT TOOK A few hours for Nott to show up at Paige's. She had forgotten that he didn't have a car and was used to hitchhiking when he had somewhere to go. Fortunately Jim realized this, and was happy to drive Nott up to Eastville from Cape Charles.

"Oh, darn, Jim! I'm so sorry. I'm just so preoccupied that I forgot Nott would need a ride."

"Paige, that's okay," said Jim. Jim was a good-looking man with silver hair and a deep water tan manifesting his life outdoors. "Gives me a good reason to stop by and see Donna at her office." He smiled. Sneak in and give her a quick peck on the cheek.

Paige and Nott stood on the wide front porch watching Jim drive off. Unobtrusively Paige scanned Nott, wondering if he was sleeping well. She hadn't seen him in several days and was concerned for his well-being. Nott wore a threadbare flannel shirt that had once been red over a grayish teeshirt and a pair of khaki cargo pants. His shaggy black curls hung over his ears. But he looked healthy, if scrubby.

"What's happening, Paige?" asked Nott, turning to her as Jim's dust settled in the crushed oyster shell driveway.

"Nott, did you hear about that skeleton they found on the breakwater ship at the ferry landing?"

"Yeah, the radio had something about it. I was listening for news about the hurricane, and they mentioned finding a body. My batteries were getting low, though, and I had to turn it off. Save it for emergencies, you know."

"Looks like we've got another unknown body," said Paige. "The Coast Guard found this one when they were investigating the fast boat crash. It's just a skeleton left with some scraps of clothes and a pair of rubber boots. It's all back in my workroom."

"No identification?" asked Nott.

"Nope," replied Paige. "No ID., no obvious sign of what killed him, no idea of who."

"Well, what do you want me to do?" he asked.

"Nott, it looks like the Coast Guard and the sheriff's department are having a little jurisdiction problem. They're not fighting over who gets the case. It's more like which one *has* to take it. And neither of them have done any crime scene investigation."

"That's not good."

"No," agreed Paige. "So if no one else is going to do it, it'll have to be us."

"Us?"

"You and me, old buddy."

"Wait a minute, Paige. I helped out before because the law thought I was involved. But I'm not a detective. Heck, I'm not even employed. Remember? I'm just a crippled geek who lives out over the inlet. I got nothing to do with this one."

Paige gave him a disappointed pout. "Well, you and I worked so well together the last time. And I thought maybe you'd feel you owed me."

"Owed you? What for?"

"C'mon, Nott. If I hadn't gotten involved you'd still be sitting over in the jail."

"Well—"

"You know that's true. I got you out of jail, and I kind of got you out of your shell, too."

"Well—"

"Who was it that got you to clean up? And got you some better clothes? And took you to church, and the church supper, and the fish fry down in Cheriton? Huh? Who?"

"You, Paige," he muttered, his head hanging down.

"So I thought you'd want to help me out in my time of need."

He laughed. "Paige, you're getting a little melodramatic, aren't you?"

She laughed too. "Yeah, I am. But I do need your help, Nott. Will you help me?"

She tried to look both pitiful and hopeful.

"Sure, Paige. I guess so. But just remember, I don't know nothing about these things. I'll just be a strong back for you."

"That's all I ask. Just that you be there with me just in case."

"Let's get going, then."

Chapter Four

WHEN THE COAST Guardsmen found the skeleton they were understandably surprised. They had some necessary equipment onboard their patrol boat, though, and after their initial surprise they unstowed their body bag. Donning Nitrile gloves and N95 masks they clambered back aboard the hulk and made their way to where the skeleton lay. Hunkering down to reach under the superstructure they pulled out the clothes and bones they could see and put them in the body bag. It was still daylight so they didn't bother to use flashlights to look for anything they missed. The guano smelled bad, and the skeleton was freaking them out, and they wanted to get done and get gone before the sun went down.

So when Paige unzipped the body bag what she found was a jumbled mess. After she verified from the sheriff's office that there had been no crime scene investigation, she knew what she had to do.

The next morning she and Nott met Donna's husband, Jim, at the dock in The Gulf at the end of Smith Beach. They had Tyvek suits, gloves, booties, particle masks, evidence bags, and a tarp they could lie on to get a better look under the superstructure. Paige had replaced the batteries in her bright tactical flashlight, brought a mirror, to look under things, and even a large Sherlock Holmesian-magnifying glass, all stuffed in a large duffel.

Jim never batted an eye as they stowed all the gear on his center console Carolina Skiff. They crossed the sandbar and ran south down the outside of the many shoals.

It was too noisy in the boat to chat. That was fine with Paige. It gave her time to think. She was headed to the location where just a few days ago her former boyfriend ... well, friend ... Senior Deputy Sheriff Pablo Gerena had crashed his Cigarette boat and died in a spectacular fireball while avoiding arrest. How had she not seen what a sleaze Pablo had been when she had dated him? *I guess I was just hungry for male attention,* she thought. *Thank the Lord I found out about him before he hurt me. And thank you, Lord, for getting me off that Cigarette boat before he crashed. Omigosh! I could have been fish food, too!* Was she ready to see the site where Pablo died? *I'm a professional. I'll compartmentalize that part. I've got enough to worry about with this new murder,* she thought.

They passed Cherrystone and Kings Creeks and Cape Charles Harbor finally arriving at the Kiptopeke State Park and the concrete ship breakwater.

"Which one do you want?" asked Jim.

"I think it's the end one, down at the southern end," replied Paige.

Nott hung bumpers over the starboard side of the boat as Jim ran down the shore-side of the ships. The Bay was fairly calm, but this allowed the ships to further calm the water for them. Jim snugged them up to the stern of the hulk and reached up and tied a line to a piece of rebar that had been exposed in the collision and explosion with the fast boat. Nott struggled into his Tyvek suit and booties and helped Paige into hers. Then, with a steadying hand from Jim, he climbed onto the gunnel of the Skiff and into the holed stern of the concrete ship. He reached down, grasped Paige's hand, and boosted her aboard. Jim passed up their duffel of equipment and they carefully headed through the interior wreckage to the weather deck.

The Thacher had been sitting on the bottom of The Bay since 1949, and storms had wreaked havoc on her. She had long since been picked clean of any souvenirs and now her weather decks were deep with guano, crumbled concrete, and the occasional fishing lure mis-cast by some hapless fisherman. They carefully skirted holes where hatches or ventilators had been and finally came to where the body had been found. This was apparent by the lack of guano in a man-shaped area on the deck.

"They didn't even put up tape," said Paige disgustedly. "Well, I brought a roll. Give me a hand and let's get this area taped off."

Once the crime scene tape was in place Paige took out her camera. "Didn't they already take pictures?" asked Nott.

"Well, they took some cell phone snapshots of the skeleton before they hauled it out, but they didn't really *photograph* it. More like sightseer pics. I would have liked to get a full series of photographs with the skeleton *in situ*, but we'll just have to make do with what we can."

Paige started with photographs of the overall scene from every angle she could reach. "I'm so glad we've got this digital camera," she commented to Nott. "I don't have to worry about having enough film or changing film in the middle of an investigation."

Nott nodded.

Once she had gotten the more panoramic site pictures Paige got down to the nitty gritty. Footprints were everywhere in the guano. She knew that these were almost certainly left by the Coast Guardsmen, but she put measuring scales down and photographed them anyway. She didn't want to take the chance of needing them then finding she didn't have them.

After the footprints Paige had Nott help her spread the plastic tarp over the guano adjacent to the overhang where the skeleton had been located. She then had him hold a bright white cardboard reflector to illuminate the darkness beneath the superstructure. After mounting a macro lens on her camera

Paige lay on her tummy to take close-ups of the deck where the skeleton had been. Her naked eye didn't see anything there, but she wanted the pictures to examine later.

Paige handed off the camera to Nott and asked him to keep the reflected light in the space. Then she took her flashlight and magnifier and slid underneath the superstructure. Grateful for the smell-deadening of the particulate mask Paige slowly wormed her way into the space, carefully examining the area before sliding over it.

"Whoa! Here's something," she said. "Give me an evidence bag."

Nott passed over a clear plastic bag with a zip top.

Paige squinted at what she had found. A silver St. Peter medallion with a broken chain. She sealed it in the bag. She'd date and tag it later.

"Was that his?" Nott asked.

Paige just shrugged, and continued to inch forward.

"Nott, give me another evidence bag and some tweezers."

He handed them over.

"I found a couple of strands of hair and a spot of blood on this projection. I'm glad I saw it. Almost banged my head into it myself. Don't know whose hair it is, but better too much evidence than not enough."

She scrooched back out from under the superstructure and stood up. "I guess that's about it. No blood, no weapons, nothing good like that. Just the pictures the medallion and some hair. Still, it's more than we had before."

Nott nodded his agreement. "Shall we pick up, now?"

"Yeah," she said. "Make sure we fold the tarp with the bird poop inside it so it doesn't get on anything. And let's leave the crime scene tape up. I don't think we missed anything, but still …"

They packed their tools and few finds into the duffel and made their way back to the hole in the ship's stern.

"Did ya find anything?" called Jim.

"Don't really know," answered Paige. "A couple of things. And I got a lot of high definition pictures which I'll want to go over closely. But there wasn't much left."

They clambered down into Jim's boat.

"I did find one curious thing, though," said Paige. "A St. Peter's medallion."

"St. Peter? The Big Fisherman himself. The patron saint of fishermen," remarked Jim.

"Yeah, I don't know if it belonged to the victim, or if it was lost there by some fisherman."

Jim cranked the motor. "Wind's picking up. There's a storm coming. Probably one of the distant feeder bands from the hurricane. Let's get out of here and back up The Gulf."

Quickly they began their run north.

"Ya think you've enough time to drop me off up Cherrystone?" asked Nott.

Jim looked at the sky and the waves. "Just," he said.

As they motored slowly through the shallows to Nott's house Paige asked, "You going to be all right out here in the storm, Nott?"

"Oh, sure," he replied. "This shack's been here since the early 1900's and no storm's taken it yet. Might lose a shingle or two but nothing I can't fix."

He laughed, "And I don't have to worry about losing my electric or water. Don't have either."

"How's your supply of candles and stove alcohol?"

"I'm good. You just hurry back to The Gulf and make sure you stay safe."

With the wind building Jim said he was anxious to get back to protected water. He normally moored his boat in Cape Charles, but with this storm coming he mentioned he'd be better off leaving it moored in The Gulf, and catching a ride with Paige.

"Sounds like a plan to me," said Paige, and they quickly motored up Savage Neck, past Smith Beach and to The Gulf where Jim was able to quickly tie off his boat to a number of well-sunk pilings.

"Tell you what, Jim," said Paige. "Call Donna and tell her to meet us at the Mallard Cove Restaurant and I'll treat y'all to dinner as payment for the ride out to the breakwater."

Jim thought it sounded good, but when he called Donna she was at her office in Eastville and told him that she had a council meeting to attend that night, so the thank-you dinner would have to wait.

Paige dropped Jim off at Donna's office and drove to the funeral home on Willow Oak Road.

In her workroom Paige again donned a Tyvek suit and Nitrile gloves to avoid cross contamination, and opened her duffel, removing the evidence bags and camera. She decided that the pictures could wait until the following day and, instead, took out the medallion. Looking at it under her magnifier she could see no blood or other evidence. Only a thick covering of guano from lying face down on the deck. She took a damp paper towel and gently rubbed the medallion to clean off the guano. Under her magnifier she saw the word STERLING embossed at the base of the back. Continuing to rub she found, in the middle of the medallion's back, scratched, not engraved, the initials J.C.D.

Chapter Five

SPECIAL AGENT TIM Hannegan drove over to The Shore to take Paige to dinner. She was afraid that the wind might close the Bridge-Tunnel and he wouldn't make it. It was supposed to be a date, but Paige was hoping to pump the FBI agent for ideas to help in her investigation into the identity of the skeletal remains found on the concrete ship.

Meeting her at her apartment on Wilkins Beach Tim said, "So, Paige, where to tonight?"

They had eaten at all of the local restaurants and Paige was feeling kind of fancy. "How 'bout Island House Restaurant up in Wachapreague?"

"If that's what you want, let's do it."

The drive up to Wachapreague was just over a half hour in a pouring rain. Fortunately Tim had a CD player in his car, and they listened to soft country ballads as they drove. Vince

Gill, The Dixie Chicks and Kenny Rogers serenaded them as Paige strategized about how she was going to turn this from a date into a working dinner.

As they pulled into the parking lot Paige said, "The restaurant was built to look like the old Parramore Island Life Saving Station out on Parramore Island." It was weathered unfinished wood with a lookout cupola on the roof. A lighted flag whipped in the stormy wind.

"Out where?"

"You know." She waved at the islands out in the water. "These are all barrier islands, and the Coast Guard used to have a station all the way out there on one of the islands. Pretty cool. It was accessible only by boat."

"No kidding—what happened to it? Is it still there?"

"No, it was abandoned a long time ago, and then back in '89 or '90 lightning hit and it burned to the ground."

"Wow! So this place is kind of a remembrance of it?"

"Well, I don't know if I'd go that far. It's just that those of us who were raised out here on The Shore have deep roots. We like to remember the old places like that. There was an old Coast Guard Station out on Cobb Island, further south, and they put it on a barge and brought it in to Oyster and set it up on land."

"What's it used for now?"

"To be honest," she said, "I don't think it's being used for anything. The Barrier Island people spent millions to bring it to shore to preserve it, but no one thought about what they'd do with it once they got it here."

"Hmmm. Sounds like something the Federal Government would do."

Paige chuckled in agreement.

Dinner was comfortable with small talk. Paige had the Island House's special crab cakes, and Tim ordered fried oysters.

"Don't overdo the dinner," Paige warned. "I've got a surprise for dessert."

Paige ordered them both Smith Island Cake for dessert.

"Cake?" asked Tim.

"Just wait."

The Smith Island Cake couldn't be called a "house specialty." It wasn't made locally, but was actually confected on Smith Island in the Chesapeake Bay in Maryland. It was brought to shore by boat, then driven down to the restaurant. This particular cake was made of ten pencil-thin yellow cake layers that were held together with chocolate fudge icing. As the waitress placed the small slices on their table Tim involuntarily said, "Wow."

The waitress laughed. "Yup," she said, "frosting with a little cake added."

"It's the state dessert of Maryland," Paige said, as she dug in.

After supper they sat sipping their coffee, watching the wind whip the water to a froth. "I really like the other side of The Shore," said Paige. "I love the sunsets."

As they sat Paige spoke up again. "Tim, is it okay if I pick your mind for a while?"

"Sure," he replied. "What's up?"

"It's this case with the skeleton. I'm just not sure where to go next."

"What's the sheriff's department doing?"

"Well," she said, "I guess they've looked through the missing persons reports in the two counties. Must not have found anything 'cause they've not said anything to me."

"Did they check the National Missing and Unidentified Persons System?"

"What's that?"

"It's a national data base run by the National Institute of Justice. Unfortunately even though it's free only a few states mandate its use, and Virginia isn't one of them. But they have a lot of services for local law enforcement."

"The only thing I'm reasonably sure of," said Paige, "is that he was a waterman."

"Now, how did you come to that conclusion?" asked Tim.

"His boots," said Paige.

"His boots?"

"I wouldn't expect you guys from the Midwest to catch it, but he was wearing white rubber boots when he died."

"And?"

"White rubber boots, especially stained and beat up ones like his, are what watermen wear. It's almost a totem for them."

"Really? I hadn't heard that."

"Yeah," she continued, "they even have a presence on Facebook, the Whiteboot Brotherhood."

"Okay, so he wore white boots. Anything else?"

"Nott and I went out to where they found the body——"

"On that decrepit old ship?"

"We were careful. But the sheriff's department hadn't done any crime scene investigation, and all the Coast Guard did was pull the skeleton out and toss it in a body bag, so we felt that we really should do something a little more thorough."

"And did you find anything the Coasties missed?"

"Actually, Mr. Smartypants, we did. Look at this." Paige passed over the evidence bag containing the medallion.

"Who is this?" asked Hannegan.

"I should think an Irish Catholic FBI man would know that," snarked Paige. "That's St. Peter, the patron saint of fisherman. And look on the back."

He turned the medallion over. "J.C.D. Do you know any J.C.D.?"

"No, not right off hand. There's a Jason Duke lives out at Smith Beach, but I'm pretty sure he's too old for this to have been him."

"Is he a waterman?"

"No," she replied. "He is retired from NOAA, though. That's close."

"Okay," said Tim. "At least it's something to go on."

Tim waved to the waitress for their check. "Well, since about the only thing you've got to go on right now is that he probably was a waterman, maybe you should start interviewing watermen to see if they know of anyone who is missing."

"I'll get started on that tomorrow."

"No," said Tim. "Ought to be a man. Watermen are more likely to talk with another man."

"Well, can you—?"

"No," said Tim. "It's not a federal case. Get Nott involved. I'm sure his schedule is open enough to fit it in," he said with a friendly smile. He liked the disabled veteran.

"Darn fool still doesn't have a cell phone. Makes it difficult to catch up with him. I guess I'll call and see if Jim Baugh can swing by his shack and scare him up for me."

"Since this case looks like it will go on for a while, why don't you have him bring his gear and bunk down in the apartment upstairs at your funeral home, again? That worked well the last time."

"Worked well, but got a lot of tongues wagging," Paige said.

"Well, you'll be at your apartment at the beach and he'll be up in town. There's really nothing for them to gossip about."

"There isn't … but they will. Oh, well. We lived through it before, we can do it again."

As they drove back down the road to Eastville and Paige's apartment, Tim commented, "And if anyone should be upset about it, it'd be me. Right?"

"Pretty possessive, Mr. G-man. And are you upset?"

"Nah, I know you and I know Nott. And I am pretty sure how you feel about the both of us. I think I'm safe."

"Hmmph. Don't get too sure of yourself," said Paige. She leaned over and gave Tim a quick peck on the cheek.

Tim smiled contentedly, as they drove out to her apartment on Savage Neck where they shared a bottle of wine and watched the lights of the large container ships moving up the channel to Baltimore.

Tim tried to see the ships with Paige's binoculars, but they were too far out and it was too dark.

"I've got an app on my computer from MarineTraffic.com that can tell you what those ships are," said Paige. "They even have photographs of a lot of them and information on where they are headed and where they are from."

"Really?"

"That one you're looking at right now is a container ship, the Zhoushan Island out of Hong Kong. It's been at anchor for a couple of days, I guess waiting for a berth to open up in Norfolk. Those foreign ships often throw junk over the side and some interesting trash can wash up on the beach. Jetsam."

"You're just a fount of knowledge, aren't you? Jetsam? I've heard the term 'flotsam and jetsam'. What's the difference?"

"Flotsam is the stuff left floating when a ship sinks. Jetsam is the stuff thrown overboard on purpose. When you've lived on The Shore all your life, and spent summers walking the beach, you get to see and learn all sorts of stuff. You take your entertainment where you can find it." Paige turned toward Tim with a smile.

"Like, did you know that horseshoe crabs blood is blue?"

"You're kidding me."

"See? Stick with me, city feller. I'll larnya some good stuff."

They sipped their wine, watched the ships and shared small talk until the bottle was empty. Then Tim stood, gave Paige a somewhat chaste kiss, although this one was on the lips, and drove home across The Bay.

Chapter Six

PAIGE NEEDED TO interview watermen. But she didn't know any. Oh, she knew Jim Baugh, but he was really a sportsman, not a waterman. She knew lots of charter boat captains from down at Mallard Cove Marina. But she just didn't know any white boot professional watermen. She didn't suppose Nott did, either, since he pretty much lived a hermit's life in his Cherrystone Creek oyster house.

She called Deputy Holland at the Northampton Sheriff's Department.

"Chris, I'm still working on identifying this skeleton. You having any luck?"

"No, Paige, not much. We've checked the missing persons reports both here and up in Accomack, and sent a query across The Bay, but no luck."

"Did you check the National Missing and Unidentified Persons System?" she asked.

"What's that?"

"It's a national database of missing persons out in Texas. They've got some scientific stuff, tests and stuff, that can help too."

"No," he replied. "We don't belong to that, and the sheriff never mentioned it."

"Well, tell him about it, and tell him it's free. We really ought to get involved there." Paige switched the phone to her other ear and flipped a page on her notepad.

"Chris, I'd like to talk to some of the local white boot watermen to see if they have any ideas, but I don't know any. Can you direct me?"

"Paige, if they don't know you, they ain't gonna talk to you. You're a 'from here,' but you're a woman. And young. And not from a waterman family. They're pretty closed mouth about their own."

"So you won't help me," said Paige. It was a statement, not a question.

"Nope," he said.

"Fine," she said shortly as she hung up the phone. She was getting better at curbing her temper. At least she didn't curse him and slam the phone down on the counter.

Now what?

Being "daddy's girl," and pretty, and Daddy having a fair amount of money, Paige had grown up on The Shore fairly protected. At school she'd see and chat with daughters of watermen, but Daddy was a professional man, and her family simply didn't socialize much with the *lower classes*. The fact that a lot of the watermen were a touch superstitious, and Paige's daddy was the undertaker, probably didn't help either. Kind of like many of the men who made their living on The Bay refusing to learn to swim or wear a life jacket, believing that if The Bay wanted them, it'd have them. They didn't want to be around a man who, when he'd shake your hand at church, would ask, "How're you feelin'?" as though he were fishing for customers to bury.

Paige's best friend, Donna, was a "come here," someone not born on The Shore but moved down and stayed, but being the executive director of Citizens for a Better Eastern Shore, and married to well-known sportsman Jim Baugh, had enabled her to meet and get to know many of the locals. Maybe Donna could help her out. Paige picked up her phone and called her.

"Donna, this is Paige. Can you meet for lunch? I've a favor to ask."

"Of course," Donna responded. "Up there or down here?" Donna lived near Cape Charles.

"If you're going to your office let's go to the Trading Company for lunch," said Paige.

"Great. See you around noon."

Driving from her bayside apartment Paige noticed that the storm had flooded the fields. *I hope that doesn't hurt the soybeans.*

Paige arrived early at the Machipongo Trading Company to make certain that she and Donna would secure a table inside.

Being right on the Highway the Trading Company was attracting a number of passing tourists as well as the locals who enjoyed their food, and the place could quickly fill up.

Paige got herself an iced latte, ordered an MTC BLT, bacon, spinach and tomato, for each of them, and took a seat in the back near the air conditioner. She was admiring the paintings by local artists on the wall when Donna came in.

"Get yourself something to drink," called Paige. "I got lunch."

Donna joined Paige at the table.

"Well, Miss Paige, just what can I do you for?" Donna asked. Donna was aware of some of the schemes with which Paige had occasionally involved herself and was a touch wary.

"Donna, I'm still working on identifying that skeleton they found at Kiptopeke. Sheriff's department checked all the missing persons reports, and they haven't come up with anything. We've got his dental, but we have no idea where to check for a match. Same with DNA. We just need *some* sort of break … some loose thread that we can pull on and try to make the whole thing unravel."

Donna laughed. "I like the knitting analogy. But what can I do?"

"Because he had white rubber boots I'm starting with the assumption that he was a waterman."

Donna nodded her head. "Okay. I can see that." She took a sip of her drink.

"So I want to talk with the local watermen and see if they have any ideas about who it might be or how he got there."

"Hmmm. But will they talk to you? I mean, you're from here, and I'm sure many of them know that or know of your father, but ... well, you're still just a girl to a lot of them."

"Yeah, I know," said Paige. "Actually, if I can identify who I want to talk to I can send Nott. He's male and scruffy and was born right here in Machipongo."

"Do you think he's up to it?" Donna asked. She remembered the Nott-of-old who lived as a hermit in his world of PTSD.

"Oh, yeah. Nott's doing okay. He'd never make it in a Toastmaster's Club, but he's fine," said Paige.

"Well, good, then. But, what can I do?"

"Donna, you know so many people around here, who do you think I should talk to?"

They continued their chat as they ate their lunches. The local tomatoes were so juicy they squirted with each bite and the crisp bacon and lettuce hit the spot. Donna would stop to call Jim, to ask his opinion, and sometimes Paige would call her friend Hayley, whose husband was a waterman, to ask her. By the time lunch was over they had settled on a list of only three for Nott to interview.

"We should have been able to come up with more names," lamented Donna.

"It's just gonna have to do," responded Paige, as they left. Donna had to get back to her CBES office and Paige needed to corral Nott and talk with him about their next steps.

Paige drove down to Cape Charles to find someone to take her out to Nott's shack and fetch him ashore. It was annoying that she had no other way to contact Nott. It wasn't like they were dating, or anything. And he wasn't working for her. And, really, his working with her in her coroner role was so unofficial as to be ludicrous. But Paige was a touch OCD. Nott was a tool that she needed, and it bugged her that she couldn't just reach out and use it. Him. Her "tool." Whatever. Besides that, she liked having him for a friend, and she felt a certain responsibility for him.

There wasn't much happening at the City Dock so she drove over to King's Creek Marina to see if she could catch a ride out with someone there.

Fortunately Sonny Long was getting his boat ready to go out fishing along the Bridge-Tunnel islands and was more than happy to run Paige up to Nott's shack. The tide was high enough that he'd not have any problems with the draft of his boat, but he couldn't wait around. That was fine by Paige. Nott still had his scow, and they could ride back together in it.

Paige hadn't considered what she'd do if Nott wasn't at his shack, but as they approached she spotted his old scow tied up to one of the support pilings. Nott heard them coming, and walked out to the steps going down to the water. He helped Paige climb out, and she waved as Sonny backed off, turned around and motored down the creek to The Bay.

Nott looked kind of confused. "Paige, what are you doing here?" he asked. "You stayin'?" After all, her ride had just left without her.

"Pack your stuff for a short stay up at the Eastville apartment," said Paige. "I need your help."

"Umm, okay."

"I left my car at King's Creek Marina. We'll run your boat in there."

"Paige, they won't let me leave my boat at King's Creek. They say it's too … decrepit."

"Oh, okay, you drop me off there to get my car and meet me at the town dock. Okay?"

Nott nodded his assent. He had acquired an old duffel bag from somewhere, and he stuffed a few clothes, his poncho liner-blanket, and his toothbrush inside, tossed it into his scow, and off they went.

Chapter Seven

NOTT HADN'T ASKED Paige what she needed his help with. He honestly didn't have a lot of curiosity. He just preferred to go with the flow, following life wherever it happened to take him. But Paige had helped him when the law had wrongly accused him of murder. And she had helped him come pretty far out of his PTSD shell. He owed her, and anything he could do to help, he would.

The outboard motor on his scow was made far too much racket for them to talk on the way into Kings Creek Marina so Nott waited until they were in Paige's car and headed up the road. He waited patiently knowing that she'd broach the subject when she was ready.

"Nott," she said, "do you know any watermen? Any of the 'whiteboot brotherhood'?"

"What do you mean, Paige?" he asked. "What do you need?"

Paige explained her theory that perhaps one of the local watermen might know of someone of their group who was missing or might have an idea of how the man on the concrete ship died. "I'm really grasping at straws, here," she said. "There's no legal paper about someone missing, and there was no ID on the body, so I just don't know where else to look."

"Is the sheriff doing anything?" asked Nott.

"I don't really know. They're doing all of the stuff their protocols dictate, checking data bases and such, but I think this is going to call for some more off-the-wall investigating."

Nott laughed softly. "Well, that's what we're good at."

Together they talked about who Nott should talk to. "Donna and Jim suggested Jack Long, the pound fisherman; Ralph Haynie, the crabber; and Tom Weisiger, the clam farmer. Do you know any of them already?" Paige asked.

"No, but if Donna or Jim will introduce me, I guess I'm game to give it a try."

Jack Long was first on the list. After Jim Baugh had called to let him know, Nott gave him a call.

"MR. LONG—"

"Jack."

"Great, Jack, I'm working with the county coroner to try to identify that skeleton they found on the concrete ship at Kiptopeke. Would you have some time to talk with me?"

"Ayah, as long as you can talk and work at the same time."

"Huh?"

"I gotta go out and fish my pounds first thing in the morning. You want to talk, meet me at the dock in Oyster round about five tomorrow morning."

"Five?" gulped Nott.

"Ayah. That's when we head out. You want to talk, you be there."

"Yessir. I'll see you then." But Long had already hung up the telephone.

The sun hadn't even begun to blush over the eastern horizon when Nott pulled the Reese Funeral Home pickup truck into Oyster the next morning. Nott had remembered to wear his old scarred white rubber boots. He found Long and two other deckhands in his forty-foot Chesapeake deadrise at the dock.

"You Nott?"

"Yessir."

"Well, get aboard. We got a lot of work to do. At least you had sense enough to wear the right boots." The fisherman nodded at Nott's white rubber boots.

Long was tall, painfully thin, and well-weathered. It was impossible to guess his age after the effects of wind and water on his face. He was dressed like Nott with heavy canvas pants, a faded flannel shirt and white rubber boots.

"I—" Nott started to answer, but Long started the old diesel engine on his boat making conversation impossible. *How am I supposed to interview him over this racket?* Nott thought to himself.

They rode out through the sandbars and shallows of the barrier islands for over thirty minutes until they came to the first of the pounds.

The pound was made of fishnet strung between pine poles sunk into the bottom. The structure created a hedge across the prevailing current to block fish schooling by. They instinctively turn away from the land and swim along the hedge until they are gathered in by winglike sweeps of net that concentrate them into a funnel. The funnel leads to the main pound enclosure, and then another funnel leads the fish into a fifteen-by-thirty-foot trap complete with a net bottom where they wait for the fishermen.

Captain Long tied his boat to a downwind stake by the main enclosure and his two hands pulled up the skiff they had been towing behind and pulled their way into the pound by the net. As they reached the trap they could see that it was seething with flashing bodies.

"Okay, Cap," they called, and Long started up the donkey engine on the back of the boat. The men in the skiff methodically pulled in the trap net, holding it with their knees against the side of the boat, concentrating the fish even more.

"Here it comes," called Long, and a huge net that looked like an overgrown dip net swung out on a boom. The mate grabbed its wooden handle and dipped it down into the writhing mass. While the second man held the line that kept the bottom of the purse-like net closed, Captain Long used the donkey engine to swing the heavy load back aboard. Then the purse was tripped, and a waterfall of fins and scales cascaded into the boat's hold.

Nott was fascinated by all this, but he still hadn't been able to talk with Captain Long about the skeleton.

After the pound had been emptied, and several hundred pounds of fish were in the hold, Captain Long shut off the donkey engine. The relative silence was deafening.

"Captain," began Nott, but Long waved him off.

"Not quite yet," he said.

He started the engine on the workboat and motored around to the other side of the pound. "D'ya see this?" he asked Nott, pointing to a place where the stake supporting the pound net was missing. "Gotta fix that or we'll lose fish."

Lashed to the side of the deadrise were several sixty-foot long pine poles. They looked like whole trees that had been stripped of their bark.

"Come on and lend a hand," said Long as he unlashed one of the poles.

They positioned the pole where the missing one had been. "They's only one way ta do it," said Long, as he lifted the pole vertically and then slammed it into the bottom.

One of the mates came over and wrapped a line around the pole, using it as a handle, and the both of them lifted the pole up a ways and then slammed it back into the bottom. It took about an hour for them to sink fifteen feet of the pole into the bottom and tie the fishnet to it.

"You have to do that for every stake?" asked Nott. "There's gotta be—"

"Round about one-hundred thirty per pound," said Long. "And we got to take them all up again end ta season if we want to use 'em again. Cain't afford new stakes ever year." The grizzled man rested a hip against the boat's gunnel.

"Okay, now, boy, what is it you want to talk to me about?"

"You can talk now?"

"Yeah. Them two gotta go down and cull them fish. Usual they do that while we run to the next pound, but I guess I can take the time to talk while they work."

Captain Long lit up a foul-smelling pipe of tobacco as the two of them sat on a gunnel.

"I guess you heard about the skeleton they found on the breakwater ship at Kiptopeke?"

"Ayah."

Nott fingered a rough line holding spare poles to the side of the gunnel. "He didn't have any identification on him, but he had been wearing white rubber boots when he died. We kind of hoped that meant that he was a waterman."

"Huh?"

"No, that didn't come out right. With nothing else to go on we kind of hoped that, since mostly watermen wear white rubber boots, that might give us a lead to finding out who he was."

"You're wearin' white boots. You call yourself a waterman?"

"No," admitted Nott. "But I do live in an Oyster Guard House up Cherrystone Creek."

Long puffed his pipe back to life. "Oh, that's who you are. I heard of you."

"So, just on the chance, you know, we're talking to some local watermen to see, you know, to see if maybe you know of anyone ... missing."

"Missing watermen?"

Nott nodded.

"Always lose a few, but usually after a big storm."

"Yeah, but, do you know of anyone missing on The Shore who just ... disappeared?"

"Oh, I see what you want." Long paused to spit over the leeward side. "You know you never spit to windward," he said with a grin. "No, can't say I know of anyone missing with no cause."

Nott nodded in resignation. "Well, I'd appreciate it if you call the funeral home if you think of anything, okay?"

"Ayah," answered Long.

They wandered over to where the other two hands were culling the fish.

"What we got, boys?"

They had been sorting the catch into different baskets. Croaker, weakfish, some flounder, mullet and a few menhaden. Then there were some trash fish, oyster toads, and the like.

"Wish there were more bunkers," said Long. "Ain't as many of them around since them big factory boats been workin' The Bay."

"Well," said Nott. "Ready to head in?"

Captain Long laughed. "You might be, but we got two more pounds to work. It's long days workin' the water."

Nott simply nodded his head as Long fired up the diesel and they started their run through the inner guts to the next fish pound. The sun was long gone when they finally returned to the dock in Oyster and Nott took his weary self up the road to the apartment above the funeral home.

Chapter Eight

WHEN NOTT GOT out of bed the next morning he felt aches in muscles he hadn't known existed. As he creakily walked to the bathroom the scents of coffee and bacon came from the kitchen. He brushed his teeth, dressed in clean blue-jeans and a work shirt, and walked barefoot out to the kitchen.

"Paige, what are you doing?"

"Fixing breakfast. You looked really bad when you got back last night, and I thought I'd help you build up your strength for tonight's action."

"Tonight?" he moaned in despair. "What's tonight?"

"I set up for you to talk to Ralph Haynie at his crab shack tonight."

"At night?"

"Yeah, he'll be working his peeler floats. He's got to work them every three hours or so, all night long, to make certain he doesn't miss any busters."

"Busters?"

"He'll explain it all to you. He left at 5:30 this morning to work his pots, so you'll need to meet him around 11:00 tonight at his place. Just take it easy today, and I'll get some work done in my office downstairs. I still have a business to run and a couple of appointments today. You want to join me?"

"Sit in while you sell someone a funeral? No thank you."

Nott spent the day reading and napping. He wasn't sure what to expect that night, but if it anything like his time working the fish pounds, it would be strenuous. Nott pulled up to Ralph Haynie's dock on a creek bayside of Cheriton just before 11:00 p.m. A long wooden walkway stretchedt over the water. Near the end of the dock was a tin-roofed shanty house with the lights on.

As Nott walked to the shack he looked at the many 3' x 12' pine crab shedding floats moored to poles alongside. Lights were suspended above the floats but they weren't turned on so he couldn't see what might be inside the floats.

Haynie poked his head from the shanty. "Hey," he called to Nott.

"Hey."

"Wait there. I'll be right out."

The lights illuminating the floats came on, startling Nott.

"C'mon," said Haynie. He stepped down into a smelly wooden skiff. Nott joined him. "Siddown. I'll learn you somptin'," said Haynie as he pulled the skiff over to the first float. "Y'ever work crabs?"

Nott allowed that he hadn't.

Haynie caught a crab in the first float and held it up to Nott. "These 'er white sign," said Haynie.

"White sign?"

"Yeah. Look at this flipper. See this? That's white sign. That means she won't shed for another ten days."

"Okay," said Nott, not really understanding. *Shed?*

"We just leave 'em in here." Using a net that looked more like a squash racket Haynie flipped each crab in the float and examined its flippers. Some he tossed back and others he placed in a basket at his feet.

"What are those?" asked Nott.

"Those're pink sign." He passed one to Nott. "See that?" He pointed to the flipper. "These'll shed in around four days. They go in that float over there." Haynie worked another several floats of white signs and when he finished he had a bushel basket of pink signs. He pulled them over to another float. "This's pinks," he said and gently dumped the bushel basket in one end, then began examining the other crabs in the float. "This's a red sign. Look." He passed the crab over. Nott could clearly see the red where Haynie pointed. "These're rank," he said. "They'll shed in just a couple of days."

After going through several of the floats of pink sign crabs Haynie pulled the skiff over to the floats closest to the shanty. "These are the rank crabs. Gotta watch 'em close. If they shed and some varmint gets in there they'll eat 'em up. Heck, other crabs'll eat 'em. Cannibals!"

"What do the crabs that have shed look like?" asked Nott.

"Them's soft crabs." Haynie dipped his net and gently slid it under a crab that looked dead to Nott. "This here is a soft-shell crab." He offered it to Nott on the net. "Careful, now."

"Is it gonna bite me?"

"No," laughed Haynie. "Just don't want you to hurt her none."

Nott took the crab. It was as soft as though its shell had dissolved and as limp as though it were dead. "Is it okay?" he asked.

"Oh, yeah. She's alive and ready to go."

They carefully went through the final floats, and whenever they found a soft crab they delicately stacked it on top of the others in the basket. When they finished, they had two bushel baskets filled with bubbling but complacent soft crabs.

Nott was so wrapped up in what they were doing he forgot, for the moment, that he was here to interview Haynie. "And you have to do this all night long?" he asked.

"Well, sometimes my wife comes out and does it. But a peeler can shed in just a few hours, and if we don't catch it while its good and soft then we got to sell it for bait. Believe me, soft crabs fetch right more than bait crabs."

"Whew. That's a lot of work. And you have to do that every couple of hours?"

"Oh, we ain't done yet," said Haynie. "Bring them on," he said pointing at the baskets of soft crabs.

Inside the shanty sat a series of waist-high work shelves.

"Watch," said Haynie. He placed a waxed cardboard box on the table and added a layer of parchment, then dried eel grass, and then a thin layer of crushed ice. He carefully placed a layer of similarly-sized soft crabs on top of the ice. He covered these with a layer of parchment, a layer of eel grass, a layer of crushed ice, and yet another layer of crabs.

"Come on," he said to Nott. "You too. Just make sure the crabs are all like-sized."

"And you fish crab pots during the day?" asked Nott amazed.

"Yep. My daddy did it before me, and his before him. It's what we do. We's crabbers."

Nott just shook his head.

"Now, you wanted to talk with me about somethin'?"

"Oh," exclaimed Nott. "I got so caught up in the crabs I forgot."

Nott told Haynie about their efforts to identify the skeleton that had been found and asked Haynie if he knew of any missing watermen.

"Nope," he said. "Aw, ever once in a while somebody'll run off with somebody's wife. Or sometime a storm'll take someone. But them's pretty standard, you know?"

"And there's none of that going on recently?"

"Naw," said Haynie. "Not that I know of."

It was now about two in the morning and Haynie had to get a few hours sleep before heading out to work his crab pots to restock his shedding floats. Nott thanked him for the education and the information and headed back up the road to his apartment in Eastville. He was exhausted, but exhilarated in learning something more about living on The Bay. But, darn, it was a hard life, either pound fishing or crabbing. He was glad neither were his jobs.

Back at the funeral home he stumbled up the stairs. He wanted to just collapse on the bed with his clothes on, but he suspected Paige would skin him alive if he did.

Chapter Nine

PAIGE'S PHONE RANG. Tim's voice came over the line. "Hey, lady! How about some supper tonight?"

"Over there or over here?"

"I'd like to eat over there," Tim replied. "Your places are so much more interesting. And ... I really want to stay away from the office."

"Why?"

"Oh, nothing bad. It's just that there's a lot happening over here, with those blasted MS-13s, again. I'd just as soon be over there where they won't call me in for anything unless it's really bad."

"Sounds wonderful to me. Come on over."

They ate dinner at The Oyster Farm at Kings Creek. With a fresh breeze and a clear sky, they opted to eat on the patio. Tim decided that since he wanted to stay local with his supper he'd start with a dozen iced raw oysters on the half-shell. He followed that with calamari and a rich she crab soup.

Before ordering Paige laughed. "Calamari? You know that's just squid, yeah?" Tim cautiously nodded. "Over here we use squid for fish bait." She laughed again.

Paige ordered a half-dozen steamed Cherrystone clams. She followed with an artichoke and spinach dip, and Bill's ESVA Clam Chowder.

The waitress took their menus and went off to put in their orders.

Since The Oyster Farm was one of the nicer restaurants Paige had worn a skirt with a shirtwaist blouse. She glanced surreptitiously at Tim. He was wearing a collared pullover shirt of a hue that brought out his blue eyes. Paige sighed inwardly.

"I'm amazed at the number of really good restaurants you have over here on The Shore," said Tim.

"That's pretty condescending," retorted Paige. "You think we're just farmers and fishermen over here? You're the one who ordered fish bait for supper."

"Whoa, don't get your back up," replied Tim. "I'm not looking for a fight. But you've got to admit, when you're driving over here, out on 13, you don't see much. No housing developments or factories—just farms. So Cape Charles is kind of a surprise."

"Just a diamond in the muck, huh?" said Paige.

"Paige, I'm trying to give a compliment here. Quit turning things around, okay?"

"Yeah, I'm sorry," she replied. "I just get kind of prickly about The Shore. When I went off to college in Williamsburg and then up to Philadelphia I thought The Shore was a backward wasteland too. Now that I've been back living here a couple of years, and involved with the people and the institutions, I can see how rich it really is."

Tim rested his elbows on the table, listening intently.

"Growing up, Cape Charles was the closest thing we had to a city, and it was still pretty much just Mason Street with an occasional store on one of the side streets. We wanted to do any serious shopping, we'd have to go across to Norfolk. But since the tourists found Cape Charles, it's really taken off."

She waved at the décor around them. "Like this restaurant. Used to be the place to eat out was Paul's over in Cheriton. And it was a combination bus stop/soda fountain/restaurant with all the ambiance of a telephone booth. Great food and great people, but definitely small town. Oh, some folk would open a little restaurant that might last for a season. I remember Charlie Matthews taking us to some place up the road where the owner 'entertained' us by taking his teeth out and pulling his lower lip all the way up to his nose."

Tim laughed loudly.

"Now we have legitimate classy restaurants like this one and the Restaurant at Mallard Cove Marina, places like the Cape Charles Coffee House, and night spots like The Jackspot at Sunset Beach."

"You sound like you work for the Chamber of Commerce."

"No, I've just grown up enough to appreciate what we've got over here on The Shore. And for dessert, I'll show you another one."

Tim paid the bill and they drove into town. Paige had him park on Mason Street, and they walked to ***brown dog ice cream***.

"An ice cream parlor?" asked Tim, amused. "And unassumingly lowercased."

"Oh, you ain't seen nothing yet," replied Paige. "They make their ice cream fresh several times a day. And they locally source the ingredients. You can't go in fixated on one particular flavor 'cause they'll change flavors throughout the day. If you like ice cream, it's heavenly."

"I'm not normally into sweets, but I like a little ice cream once in a while."

"Come on," said Paige, "let's go in and see if Foster is here."

"Foster?" asked Tim.

"Foster. He's the original brown dog of ***brown dog ice cream***."

They entered the front door of the shop and were greeted by a huge chocolate-colored Labrador Retriever. "Tim, meet Foster," said Paige.

Foster greeted Tim with a traditional Labrador Retriever salute—a nose in the crotch while his weaponized tail beat a rapid tattoo on a nearby chair. Easing the nose out of his crotch, Tim squatted down and roughly scratched Foster behind his floppy ears pulling his wide blocky head until they were nose-to-nose. Foster licked Tim's nose, and he laughed with delight.

"Oh, I'm glad you like dogs," breathed Paige.

"Love 'em," Tim replied. "And the bigger the better."

Another tally in the 'plus' column for Tim.

They each bought a cone—Paige the *coastal roasting coffee* flavor and Tim the *raspberry chocolate chip*. Grabbing a handful of napkins, they headed down the sidewalk toward the beach and the fishing pier.

It was beginning to get late so they walked out on the pier to watch the water and wait for the sunset.

"Eastern Shore sunsets are magnificent," said Paige.

They stood shoulder-to-shoulder and watched as the sky started to turn a dark rose. Several billowing cumulus clouds added to the palette, glowing brightly where the setting sun caught them, but glowering darkly where they remained in shadow. Paige had seen vista like these literally hundreds of times before, but the majesty still virtually took her breath away. Caught up in the beauty of the moment Paige reached out and took Tim's hand. He quickly put his arm around her and they both stood transfixed as the sun finally broke free below the clouds on the horizon and seemed to spread out, melting into the waters of The Bay.

They stood there like that, not saying anything until Paige took a shuddering breath. "Wow!"

Tim agreed. "Yeah."

As the twilight faded they stood on the end of the pier watching the water and the sky. "What's that?" asked Tim, looking to the north. Lights were moving out on the water.

"Oh, that's a bunker boat," said Paige.

"Bunker boat?"

"A commercial fishing boat. About 200 feet long. They purse seine menhaden. Mossbunkers."

"Aren't they pretty close to shore there?"

"They are supposed to stay three miles out, I think. Maybe they're just anchoring for the night."

Just then they heard the rumble of an old diesel engine out on the water, and a Chesapeake deadrise hove into view with around six men aboard.

"What's that?" asked Tim. "They been fishing?"

"Well, yes and no," replied Paige. "Those are men who work on that bunker boat. It's home ported over near Norfolk, but they want to live here on The Shore, so Friday night that deadrise works as a taxi, picking the men up and bringing them ashore. Then either late Sunday or real early Monday they take them back out. It's cheaper than paying the toll across the Bridge-Tunnel and lets them live where they were raised."

As they watched the deadrise put in to the Cape Charles dock and a bunch of scruffy men climbed out. They were all wearing canvas pants and filthy white boots. A few had yellow plastic hardhats and others, dirty trucker's caps.

"Must be a tough commute in bad weather," observed Tim. They watched the men climb into an assortment of old pickup trucks and drive off. "Have you thought about your skeleton maybe being one of them? They all wear white rubber boots."

"You're right," said Paige. "I'll have to figure out how to get to talk with them. They're headquartered on the other side of The Bay. Hmm."

They walked back to Tim's car and drove to Paige's apartment at Wilkins Beach. From her window, they glimpsed the bunker boat again but it looked so close that Tim thought he could throw a rock and hit it.

"Things look a lot closer over the water," said Paige, as she brought them both some late harvest red dessert wine.

Tim sipped his. "Is this local?" he asked.

"Yeah," said Paige, "I try to stay local with as much stuff as possible. If you don't like it I've got some beer from Cape Charles Brewery in the 'fridge."

"No, I like it," said Tim. "I was just curious."

They went out to the balcony overlooking The Bay and sat in the dark sipping their wine and watching the lights out on the water.

"Okay," said Tim. "This one right on top of us is the bunker boat. What are those lights way out there?"

"Oh, they're buoys or lighthouses. Watch right over there. That one's called Wolf Trap, and it's almost all the way over on the other side. It's an actual lighthouse that marks a shoal area. It's for sale, if you're interested."

"No, I don't think so."

"And those others are buoys marking the channel to Baltimore. When I was a kid there used to be a horn buoy out there, and on very quiet nights you could hear its moan. Neat."

"Must've been a great childhood growing up here."

"Hmmph. All I could think about was getting away. I guess that's the way it is with everyone. The grass always seems greener."

"At least until you realize that it's only greener because that's where the septic tank is."

She laughed and playfully punched him on the arm.

On top of the wine at dinner, and the wine they were sipping now, they were both getting very ... relaxed.

"I'd better get going," said Tim. "I've still got to drive all the way back to Virginia Beach, and if I have any more of this wine, I'll never make it."

"You could always stay here," said Paige coyly as she looked him in the eye.

She watched him dreamily contemplate the proposition. "No, Paige, I'd better go."

She nodded in subdued understanding, and Tim slipped out the door. Paige stood for a minute leaning back against the door, then returned to the balcony and took a long hot soak in her outdoor shower, feeling the cool breeze and gazing up at the winking stars.

Chapter Ten

SHE AWOKE TO the ringing of her cell phone early the next morning. *Where the heck did I leave that phone,* she thought. She looked around the room at her clothes spread around, hanging on chairs and tables. *There it is.* She found her phone in the back pocket of her khaki pants.

"Heyo?" she slurred.

"Paige? That you? Is Paige Reese there, please?"

"This is Paige. What time is it, Nott?"

"Oh, Paige. Hey. It's a little after seven."

"Seven?" she groaned. "Whaddya want? D'you know what time it is?"

"Yeah. I just told you."

"Oh, yeah. Well … wait a minute. Lemme go wash my face."

Paige staggered into her bathroom where she peed, brushed her teeth and threw some water onto her face. *That's better,* she thought. *Now I can think straight.*

"Nott, you still there?"

"Yes, ma'am."

"Okay, what do you want?"

"Paige, we've still got to talk with that clam farmer at Smith Beach. I didn't know if you'd set that up yet, or when I need to be there."

"Oh. Right. Well, the guy you are going to talk with is Tom Weisiger. He said that if he's not in his office, they can reach him on the radio and he'll be there in fifteen or twenty minutes. So it's pretty much at your discretion."

NOTT STILL HAD access to the funeral home's pickup so after eating some cereal for breakfast he drove down Savage Neck Road to Smith Beach. It was less than a ten-minute drive. He drove down the mile-long strip of beach road to where it ended at The Gulf, and parked by the large white building that was the headquarters of the clam farm.

Stepping up into the building Nott's senses were assaulted by a variety of inputs. The complexity of the equipment overwhelmed him with pipes and pumps and pans everywhere. As complicated as it all seemed to Nott, it still had a Rube Goldberg-look to it as it was predominantly crafted from white PVC pipe. There was a lot of duct-tape engineering in evidence.

"Hello," Nott called. "Mr. Weisiger?"

A salty-looking middle-aged man in dirty khaki trousers a torn t-shirt and white rubber boots popped his head out from behind a large vat that looked like it was full of green soup.

"Hey, young man. You must be the fellow Paige Reese called me about. Welcome to the future."

Nott looked around him. The future seemed to have an awful lot of plastic pipe in it.

"Sir, can we talk?" Nott asked.

"No," replied the man.

Nott was taken aback. "But ..."

"Not yet, I mean. And call me Tom. I've got some chores to do before I can give you my full attention. You ever see an operation like this before?"

"Well, no," Nott answered slowly.

"Aquaculture. It's the future of feeding our country. The world, actually."

"You're going to feed the world on clams?" asked Nott.

"Now don't be getting silly," said Tom. "I just mean that once all of the arable land is either under cultivation or destroyed by overpopulation, we're going to have to turn to the water for the majority of our sustenance."

The man waved at the structures around him. "Take these clams, for instance. Used to be that the small edible clams like ours were difficult to find without wrecking the environment. Oh, there used to be the big dredgers out of Oyster who'd go out and dredge the Atlantic clam out in the deep water. But they'd go after the big clams they could process for Howard Johnson's clam strips and the like. The ones too tough to eat raw on the half-shell. Well, we can grow them like that, if we want. And we can do it in such a way that it doesn't tear up the bottom and kill other stuff, like crabs and flounder. But even better we can grow the smaller, Cherrystone-sized clams ... pretty much to order."

Nott had never eaten a clam in anything but a fried fritter, so he didn't know whether to be impressed or not. "Big market for those?" he asked.

Tom didn't answer, but waved Nott further into the building.

"We were some of the first to do it out here on The Shore so we kind of had to start from scratch and do it all," said Tom. "A lot of the more recent farmers buy their seed clams and all, but we do it all."

Nott was beginning to get interested. "What do you mean?"

"Do you know how clams get started?" asked Tom. When Nott shook his head, he went on. "Just like us they start with male sperm and female eggs. But with clams, they just let them flow in the water and hope that the egg and sperm hook up." Tom grinned a crooked smile.

"Well, here we know how to take our brood stock in the spring and put them into special tanks where the fertilization takes place. We don't let luck play as big a chance. Once we have this soup of fertilized eggs, we run it over into another tank where we tightly control the temperature and salinity of the water, and we pump in algae that we grow ourselves for them to feed on. That was that green stuff you saw when you first came in."

Nott was getting into it now. "So you're kind of like a nursery."

"Right! We baby these things along while they grow, at this point they're called *zygotes*, until they begin to get some size to them. The way we can tell is that we run them through a sieve. If they're of a size to get caught, we switch them to yet another tank where we feed them plankton."

"Couldn't they fend for themselves out in the water?" asked Nott. "It'd be a lot easier."

"Yeah, but we'd lose too many to fish and crabs. They don't have much of a shell yet." Tom stretched his arms over his head. "When they get big enough, about an inch across, we plant them out in the field. Sounds just like farming, don't it? They are still prime to be et by predators, so we put them in these big mesh bags like those over there. The mesh is open enough that the water and the nutrients can get through, but tight enough to keep out the crabs and oyster toads."

"Wow," said Nott, gazing around. "I never guessed."

"We go out to the planting fields every day to check on the bags and the size of the clams, and when they get to the right size we haul up the bags, empty out the clams and put them in another tank, right over here, for a few days until they've rinsed all the sand out."

Tom led Nott over to another large tank filled with clams about three inches long with a steady flow of water washing over them. He reached in and pulled out a clam.

"Here," he said as he took a knife from his belt and quickly shucked the clam.

Nott just stood there and looked at it. "What?"

"You eat it."

"Raw?"

Tom laughed. "Of course raw," and he tipped the clam into his mouth, chewing appreciatively.

"No, I don't think so," said Nott. "Thanks, anyway."

Tom swallowed his mouthful. "I remember when my Uncle Carl and I would go clamming on the sandbar just outside The Gulf. Used rakes. He'd bring up one about this size, and throw it forcefully into the basket, making sure the shell was cracked on the bigger clams. Then he'd say, 'Oh, look. That one broke,' and he'd slurp it down."

Nott shivered at the thought. He wondered who had been the first person to look at that gelatinous mess and think, *I think I'll eat that.*

"Tom," he said, "I really do need to talk to you about some important stuff."

"Sure," said Tom. "We'll talk while we check out the fields."

They walked out back of the building to where Tom kept a twenty-foot Chincoteague scow moored. Climbing in and pushing off Tom gave the fuel ball a squeeze, grabbed the starter rope on the outboard Evinrude and gave it a pull. Again the racket was far too much for them to talk, so Nott waited until they motored out of The Gulf and north to where some of Tom's clam fields were.

As they cleared the headland coming out Nott glanced south. "Tom! Are those bunker boats?"

"Yep."

"Aren't they awful close to the beach?"

"Well, distances over water are deceiving, but they sure look awful close in to me." He brought the scow to a halt.

"Do they ever bother your clam beds?" Nott asked.

"Not usually," said Tom. "Sometimes, though, they'll stir up the bottom so bad from being too shallow that the beds'll silt over. Then we gotta come out and make certain the clams don't suffocate."

"Hmmm. They look pretty intrusive to me."

"As long as we're stopped, Tom, I wanted to tell you what I'm working on with Paige as she's the coroner."

Nott explained the entire situation to Tom, and asked if he had any ideas.

"No, sorry. Don't know anyone missing. All my gang's accounted for. Don't really mix much with others, so I just don't know. Can see how it'd bug you, though."

Just then the bunker boat seemed to vomit a flow of water and fish into The Bay.

"Bycatch," said Tom.

"What?"

"Them's the fish they vacuumed up that they don't want. They're just after bunkers, menhaden. Everything else goes back."

"Are they still alive?"

"Nope. Not usually. Get in too close and they'll all wash up on the beach for people to have to deal with."

"That's pretty nasty."

"You want to know more about that, you oughta talk with Jason Duke up the beach. He's retired NOAA and has been cussing them bunker boats since he was a kid. You go see him. He'll tell ya."

Chapter Eleven

THE NEXT MORNING Paige was in her workroom with a client (read: dead body) when she heard the front screen door open then close in rapid succession. She wasn't expecting anybody, so she quickly cleaned herself up and hurried to the lobby. There was no one there. On the carpet, just inside the door, lay a business envelope with her name printed on it in block letters: **PAGE REESE**.

Idiots, she thought, *can't even spell my name right.*

Opening the envelope she found a page of lined paper that looked like it had been ripped out of a child's theme book. The message was printed in capital block letters, also.

LET THE DEAD REST IN PEACE.

Hey, thought Paige, *that'd make a snappy motto for the funeral home. Let the dead rest in peace. Yeah, I like it.*

But what did it mean? And who was it from? Paige went over all the funerals that Reese Funeral Home had performed in the past couple of months. They were all local folk, who had died of natural causes. And their people, their families, had participated in the planning and execution of the funerals. Paige just couldn't imagine who would be upset enough to pull this trick.

Nott came down the stairs. "Did someone just come?" he asked. "I thought I heard the front door."

"You heard it," replied Paige, "but this is all there was." She held out the envelope and note.

Nott looked at the envelope. "Your name's spelled wrong."

"I know that. But look at the note."

He read the note. "What's that mean?" he asked.

"I don't know."

"Did you tick someone off who just had a funeral here?"

"Not that I can think of," she replied. "I don't know what to make of it."

"Well, it can't be too important if they didn't make it clear what they wanted. I'd forget about it."

"Yeah." But Paige couldn't just forget about it. It was too weird. She went into her office and locked the envelope and note in the top drawer of her desk.

"So, Nott," she said. "How'd your visit to the clam farm go? Get anything we can use from Tom?"

"Man, that is some operation he's got out there. You ever see it?" And Nott proceeded to spend the next thirty minutes telling Paige the ins and outs of clam farming, much to her dismay. To her it was kind of like asking someone "How're you feeling?" and then having them actually *tell* you in excruciating detail, as if you really cared. But Nott was coming out of his PTSD shell, and she didn't want to do anything to mess up or slow down that progress.

When Nott finally wound down Paige said, "Yeah, but did you learn anything that might help our investigation?"

"Oh," he answered. "No."

Paige deflated further.

"Well, what're you going to do this afternoon?" she asked.

"I thought I'd catch a ride down to Cape Charles and go back out to my house," said Nott.

"Why on earth do you want to go back to that shack when you've got the use of a perfectly good apartment right here?"

"'Cause it's mine," said Nott. "It's where I got all my stuff. It's where I feel ... myself."

Paige shook her head bemused. "Okay. Well, I've got this body to prepare so I can't drive you down. Least not until tonight."

"That's okay. I'll hitch. Now I'm cleaned up, I can hitch pretty good."

"Be careful," said Paige, and as Nott went up the stairs to grab what little belongings he'd brought to the apartment, she returned to her workroom.

At about three in the afternoon she got a call from Tim on her cell phone.

"Hey, country girl. What's shaking?"

Paige smiled. "Hello, Yankee boy. You spending my tax money well?"

Tim snorted a laugh. "I thought maybe I'd come over and spend some of that tax money on my favorite tax payer. You wanna go out for dinner?"

"Sure. Want me to meet you at The Jackspot? We can drink exotically and watch the sun go down before we eat."

"You don't want me to pick you up at your apartment?" asked Tim.

Paige wondered if he was thinking about the last time they were there alone. "No," she said. "I'll meet you."

Sounding a bit disappointed Tim agreed. "See you there around 1800."

"Roger that," she replied.

Humming happily, Paige went back to work on the cosmetic reconstruction of the body on her work bench.

Later, as Paige headed out for her apartment she stopped in her office and retrieved the letter from her desk. *Maybe I'll see what Tim thinks about this,* she thought, and she stuffed the letter in the pocket of her khakis.

As she looked through her wardrobe at her beachside apartment Paige found herself humming pleasantly once again. She was looking forward to a fun evening with her dream FBI agent.

She shimmied into a pair of starched and ironed blue jeans buttoned up a crisp white Oxford-cloth shirt. Playfully she pulled on a pair of tooled cowboy boots, and a western Stetson to finish the look. She stepped back and looked in a full-length mirror attached to the back of her bathroom door. *Yeah. That's the look.*

She timed her departure so she'd arrive fashionably late at Jackspots. She wanted to make an entrance. Stepping out onto the Bayside patio fifteen minutes late, knowing that Tim would be painfully punctual, she let the heels of her cowboy boots click loudly on the pressure-treated boards. Conversation stopped and heads turned to check her out as she passed, heading for the table where Tim sat. He noted the silence and turned to see what was causing it. When he saw Paige his jaw dropped. He fumbled, rising from his seat and pulling a chair out for Paige, his mouth still hanging open.

As she reached the table Paige reached up and pushed Tim's mouth closed. Then she slid the hand behind his head and pulled his lips to her own. "Howdy, cowboy," she purred as she released him and pulled back. She smiled at him as she demurely sat in her chair. "Tim? You gonna join me?" she asked.

Tim dropped into his chair. "Wow!" he managed to say.

"Hmmm?" she asked.

"Wow!" he said again. "You look … really great."

"Oh, thank ya, kind sir," she drawled in a fake Texas accent. Then she laughed. "I just thought I'd give this outfit a try and see how you liked it."

Tim still hadn't blinked. "I wish there were a place over here to go line dancing. Maybe next week you can come over to Virginia Beach and we can go to The Eagle's Nest."

"The Eagle's Nest?"

"Yeah. The full name is The Eagle's Nest Rockin' Country Bar. They're in Chesapeake. We go over there, drink some long necks and do some line dancing."

"You're on. That sounds like a lot of fun."

"Great." Tim looked like he was looking forward to that.

They had a wonderful seafood dinner of Bay crab cake sandwiches with red pepper mayo. Tim had a draft of Cape Charles Cobb Island IPA and Paige a Jackspot margarita. They sipped their drinks and watched as the sun dropped to the horizon.

"Tim, can I show you something that came today?" Paige pulled the letter out of her back pocket and passed it over to Tim.

Tim took the envelope gingerly by its corner and looked at her questioningly.

"Somebody opened the front door, dropped that on the rug, and then left."

"Okay." Tim reached into his pocket and pulled out a pair of black Nitrile gloves. "Has anyone else seen this?"

"I showed it to Nott," she said.

Using gloved fingers Tim slipped the notepaper out and unfolded it on the table.

LET THE DEAD REST IN PEACE.

"What does that mean?" he asked.

"I really don't know," Paige replied. "I haven't had any problems with the business. And I don't know anyone who's angry with me for anything."

Tim thought, biting his lip. "How about any problems with your coroner stuff?"

"Oh. I hadn't thought about that. No, the only thing there is that skeleton. And we don't have any idea who it is. Doesn't look like we're going to find out, either. I can't imagine this has anything to do with that."

"Well," said Tim, "it doesn't look like a practical joke. Did you ask Nott about it?"

"Yeah, he was there when it came. He didn't have any idea, either."

"Paige," said Tim, "if we can't come up with anything else, we've got to assume that it's not just a joke."

"What do you mean?" asked Paige, losing her fun-high and beginning to grow worried.

"Paige, I admit that as a Special Agent I tend to be a bit paranoid. But always being prepared for the worst means never getting blindsided by bad surprises."

"Yeah, but that's a horrible way to go through life. Always expecting the worst of everybody? That's not living."

"Cowgirl, sometimes those injuns are looking for scalps, not cigars."

"What? Quit with the metaphors. What are you talking about?"

"Paige, I'm just saying that being prepared means … crap, being prepared. Not getting surprised. No, I'm not saying to distrust everyone. Just make sure that you don't blow off things that are questionable. Be prepared."

"Okay," she said quietly.

"Paige, I don't want to sound overly suspicious, but, at least for the next little while please be careful. Be cautious. I don't know what this might be, but I worry for you, so please, if not for yourself take care of yourself for me. Okay?"

"Okay. I'll 'watch my six,' Tex."

Chapter Twelve

WITH NOTHING ELSE to do Nott took his scow and motored out of Cherrystone Creek and into The Bay. A fortuitous atmospheric high had turned the approaching hurricane before it even hit Hatteras and sent it skittering along the Gulf Stream toward Bermuda. The weather in The Bay was fine.

Heading north he made his way up Savage Neck until he reached Smith Beach. He wanted to follow Tom Weisiger's suggestion to talk with Jason Duke about the bunker boats.

As he motored north he glanced to his left. There, way out on the horizon, a small airplane circled low. It was a spotter for one of the bunker boats. The airplane would look for a school of menhaden large enough to be of interest and radio the coordinates to the ship it was supporting.

Nott continued up the beach until he reached a mooring in front of Jason Duke's cottage. He hadn't called ahead, so he hoped that Duke was in. He climbed the stairs from the beach and found a septuagenarian sitting on a small wooden deck at the top in a weather-beaten Adirondack chair.

"Cap'n Duke?" asked Nott.

The old man had a full beard and long thick wavy hair, both mostly gray shot through with occasional strands of black. His face had the leathery look of someone who had stood on the weather deck of too many ships over too many years, and his eyes were a washed-out blue. He was dressed in khakis washed almost white and a white t-shirt. On his head he wore a ballcap that once had been red but now was bleached and stained and of a nondescript color.

He didn't rise, but looked up at Nott and growled, "What can I do for you, son?"

"Cap'n, I was out with Tom Weisiger in his clam fields the other day, and I asked him about the big commercial fishing boat that looked like it was almost on the beach a mile or so south of your place here."

Duke nodded his head.

"Weisiger said they were 'bunker boats,' and that if I wanted to know anything about them I should talk with you."

Duke turned his head and spit over the bank down into the weeds growing on the bank. "Uh, huh. Talk to me about what?"

"Like I said, the boat looked awful close to the beach. He said that you had some heartburn with that."

"Heartburn? Crap! It's a lot more than that. We used to be able to go out here fishing in an old scow and fill a peach basket with croaker and weakfish and swellin' toads. Even could catch some really big flounder. Big flounder! Then them bunker boats came in and started purse seining everything up, and our fishing went to hell."

"You're saying that the sport fishing out front here fell off because of the bunker boats?"

"They deny it, but I can only tell you what I've seen in my seventy-plus years." He leaned back in his chair.

"Not only that. Let me tell you, I see two or three of these factory ships operating in only fifteen to twenty feet of water less than a mile off our beach each week. I used to dive in that area watching the bottom feeders and coral formations. They're all gone now. Those seine nets have torn it all up. And without that habitat for the fish and crabs to grow, the fishing and crabbing are shot."

"Yeah, I can see that," said Nott.

Duke pursed his lips. "Then there's the problem of the bycatch."

"The what?"

"Bycatch. When they put out that net they bring up a lot more than just the menhaden. They catch bluefish, rock fish, croakers, weakfish, even flounder. They ain't supposed to. The law says that if they catch too many recreational fish in a net they're supposed to let the net go. Problem is by the time they get the fish into the hold to see what else they've caught, it's too late. The other fish are either dead or hurt too bad to live. That's bycatch."

"Man, that's bad."

Duke stood up. "You wanna beer?" he asked stepping into his house. He came out with six bottles, putting four into the cooler as he sat back down in his Adirondack chair.

Nott nodded his thanks and cracked open the bottle. "I was out working fish pounds with Jack Long the other day. He said something about how he no longer caught any menhaden in his nets."

"Ain't none left after the bunker boats get through."

"Sounds like they're more trouble than worth," said Nott.

"And that's just when things are working right for them. They'll sometimes have torn nets or something goes wrong mechanically and they dump thousands of dead fish into the water. Then we've got a major cleanup problem on the beaches."

Nott took a deep swallow of his beer. "But aren't they regulated?" he asked.

Duke snorted. "Regulated? Hmmph. Money talks. Virginia is the only state that allows bunker boats to operate in their bays. They set limits, but the company says the limits aren't reasonable and go way beyond them. And nothing is done about it."

"I can see why you're upset."

"Yeah. And it's big business, so they get away with it. Their lobbyists pour money into politics. And you know how it is in politics—money talks."

The two of them sat there drinking their beers and contemplating the inequities of the world.

"What got you started on this?" asked Duke.

"You got another beer?" asked Nott, and Duke reached down into the cooler at his side retrieving two bottles dripping from the ice water in the container.

As they drank their fresh beers Nott told Cap'n Duke about the skeleton found on the concrete ship at Kiptopeke. He told him how the victim had apparently been wearing white rubber waterman's boots, and that was why they were talking with other watermen to see if they knew of anyone who had gone missing.

"Havin' any luck?" asked Duke.

"Not a bit," replied Nott. "You have any ideas, Cap'n?"

"No, don't know 'bout anyone gone missing. You try across The Bay?"

"Yeah, the sheriff's department worked that possibility. And Paige Reese, the coroner? She's even talked with an FBI agent she knows over in Virginia Beach."

"Didn't turn up nothing?"

"Nope."

Nott wiped the bottle's perspiration on his pant leg. "Did find a St. Peter's medallion under the skeleton. Had the initials JCD scratched in the back. But that hasn't led anywhere, either."

Duke's eyes went wide. "JCD? That's my initials."

Nott perked up.

"But I'm a Methodist. I don't wear a saint's medallion. Sorry, son. Not me."

Nott was disappointed, but by this time civil twilight was coming on. "Well," said Nott, "I'd better get back to Cherrystone before it gets too late."

Shaking Duke's calloused hand, he said, "Cap'n, thanks so much for the talk and the education. Let Paige know if you think of anything, okay?"

As he motored back south to his house on Cherrystone Creek Nott looked west and could see one of the big factory fishing boats heading for The Shore. "Damn things," he thought, and continued on home.

Chapter Thirteen

IT WAS NINE fifteen in the morning and Donna was sitting by herself at a table in the Cape Charles Coffee House. She looked at her watch. Paige was forty-five minutes late, and Donna was getting concerned. Digging her cell phone out of her satchel she called Machipongo Trading Company.

"Machipongo Trading. How may I help you today?" came the greeting.

"Susie, this is Donna Bozza. Is Paige Reese there?" They'd often go to Machipongo Trading for breakfast or lunch. Maybe one of them misunderstood today's plans.

"No, ma'am, Miss Donna. I haven't seen her today. Is there something wrong?"

"No, thanks, Susie. No problem."

"Okay then. Y'all oughta come in for lunch today. We've got some fresh softshells in this morning."

"Great. Thanks."

So, she wasn't still up in Eastville.

She called the Northampton County Sheriff's office.

"Northampton Sheriff," answered Maddie the dispatcher.

"Hey, Maddie. This is Donna from CBES. I'm waiting for Paige Reese down in Cape Charles and she's forty-five minutes late. Are there any accidents out on the highway?"

"No, ma'am. No accidents or traffic anywhere in the county that I know of."

"Okay, Maddie. Thanks."

She dialed Paige's cell phone again. It went straight to voice mail.

What to do? Paige wasn't like this. She kept her dates, and always called if she were going to be late. Donna was getting worried.

She called Pam Kellam the postmistress. "Pam, Donna. Have you seen Paige today?"

"No, what's up?"

"She's an hour late meeting me at the Coffee House and I'm getting worried. Can you get someone to cover for you and check up at her office?"

Pam agreed. A short while later Pam called Donna and reported that there was no sign of their friend. The funeral home was closed up tight.

"What about at her apartment at the beach?"

"Donna, I'm sorry. I can't get out there to check."

"That's okay. I've got to head up to my office in Eastville anyway. I'll go by way of her apartment and see if she's there."

"You let me know."

Donna hopped in her car and headed up the road. She was worried. *Where are you, girl?* she thought.

She pulled into the mostly empty parking lot at the Bill Reese complex at Wilkins Beach. *There! There's Paige's car.*

Donna went up to Paige's apartment and knocked. Nothing. She knocked louder. Still no answer.

Paige had given Donna a key to her apartment so she let herself in.

As she closed the door behind her Paige's huge Maine Coon cat, Pongo, came up and vociferously let her know that he was not happy.

"Pongo! Where's Paige?" asked Donna. "Paige?" she called loudly.

The drapes looking out over The Bay were open, and the apartment was brightly lit. Donna went into the kitchen, followed closely by Pongo, still complaining bitterly.

"No wonder you're upset; you don't have any water." Donna filled Pongo's water bowl and put it down for him. The cat still complained. "Okay, okay, quit cursing." Donna opened a can of wet cat food, emptied the glutinous mess onto a saucer and placed it next to the water bowl. That shut the cat up as he started gorging on the food.

"I fed Pongo," called Donna as she went further into the apartment. "Paige?" Still no answer.

Now feeling scared as well as worried Donna went into Paige's bedroom. The bed was unmade and there were clothes strewn in the floor as though dropped there while Paige was preparing for bed.

Querulously, now, Donna called out, "Paige?" as she gingerly opened the bathroom door, half expecting to find Paige lying on the floor. She wasn't sure whether she was relieved or disappointed to find the bathroom empty, as well.

By now Pongo had finished his dinner and was back rubbing against Donna's leg, looking for attention.

She sat on the couch and Pongo hopped up next to her. "Pongo, where'd she go?" The cat merely sat and licked his paw with studied disinteret.

Donna locked the apartment and returned to her car. She didn't have any cell phone coverage out here, so she drove on into Eastville to the sheriff's office.

The desk sergeant looked up as she entered. "Hey, Miss Donna! Did you find your friend?"

"I need to see the sheriff."

"Sorry, ma'am, but he's across The Bay for the day. Can I help you?"

"I want to file a missing person's report."

The deputy sat up straighter. "Beg your pardon, ma'am?"

"Paige Reese is missing. She's not at her office and I just came from her apartment and she's not there. Her car is, and her cat is, but she's not. I want to make an official report."

"Yes, ma'am. How long has she been missing?"

"Umm, well, she was supposed to meet me for breakfast this morning ..."

The deputy shook his head. "I'm sorry, Miss Donna, but you know someone isn't missing until it's been twenty-four hours. Maybe she's gone to visit family."

Donna's worry turned to agitation. "Deputy, I told you her car is at her apartment. And her cat was left in her apartment with no water or food."

"Well, yes ma'am, but still, if she's only been missing since breakfast—"

"No, I told you we were supposed to meet for breakfast. Who's to say she didn't disappear last night?"

"Even then. It's not been twenty-four hours. We can't do anything official until it's been twenty-four hours."

"But—"

"No, sorry. Nothing we can do. She'll show up. And if she doesn't, just come back in tomorrow and we'll take an official statement then. Sheriff'll be back then, too."

Donna stomped out of the office, slamming the door behind her.

She drove to the post office. "Pam," she said, "I just came from Paige's apartment. She's not there. Pongo was really hungry. And her car is parked in the lot."

"Did you go in?"

"Yes, she gave me a key. That's how I knew Pongo was there. But she wasn't."

"Was there any sign of trouble?" asked Pam, a concerned look on her face.

"Her clothes were spread on the floor of her bedroom, and her bed was rumpled, but, well, that's just Paige. I didn't see anything else."

"Strange," agreed Pam.

Donna drove over to her CBES office adjacent to the old court house. Picking up her office phone she called information for the number of the Norfolk Field Office of the FBI.

"Tim Hannegan, please," she said when the phone was answered. She waited.

"Special Agent Hannegan."

"Tim, this is Donna Bozza ... Paige's friend?"

"Sure, Donna. What can I do for you?"

"Umm, I'm not really sure how to ask this. Is Paige over there with you?"

"Huh, wish she were," he joked. "What's up?"

"Tim, she was supposed to meet me for breakfast in Cape Charles this morning, and she never showed up."

"Did she forget?"

"I tried calling her, and her cell phone goes straight to voice mail."

"Well, maybe she forgot to turn it on this morning."

"I went to her apartment out at the beach and had our friend Pam go by her office. Nothing. Her car is parked at her apartment. I've got a key so I let myself in. Her cat is there, and he didn't have any water or food, but no sign of Paige. Tim, this just isn't like Paige, and I'm getting worried."

"Could she have gone over to another friend's house? Or gone to visit relatives?"

"No, like I said—her car is at her apartment. And she left her cat alone. Tim, I'm worried."

"Did you talk with the sheriff's department?" asked Tim.

"Yeah," she responded, disgust edging her voice. "They won't do anything until tomorrow."

"True. Well, Donna, you know this isn't anything federal. There's nothing I can do officially."

"I know," said Donna. "But I'm worried, and I was kind of hoping you might have heard from her."

"Not a word. I'll tell you what, Donna—I'll come over tonight when I get off work here. Can I meet you at your office and you can let me into the apartment?"

"Sure."

"And how about the funeral home?" he asked.

"Well," said Donna, "I suppose I'll have to call her brother Billy to get off his fishing boat and do some work. It'll be good for him."

"And I'll be able to get in to look around? Tell Billy that if he sees anything *hinky* to just leave it alone and wait for me to get there."

"Okay," said Donna. "Please get over here as early as you can."

Chapter Fourteen

TUESDAY AFTERNOON.

BLACK. DARKNESS. *AM I awake? Am I alive? Is this what it feels like to be dead? Whew! If so Heaven smells terrible.*

Paige's eyes were closed. She couldn't open them No. They were stuck shut. *Why can't I open my eyes?*

She tries turning her head. It turns, but only so far. And there's nothing to see. As well as her eyes being stuck shut, there's something covering her head. *What's this over my head? Why does it smell so strange?*

She starts to panic. *What's happening to me? Why is it happening to me? Where am I?*

Paige tries to reach up to feel her eyes. *I can't move my arms. Why can't I move my arms? How am I supposed to fix my eyes if I can't move my arms?*

Panic advancing, Paige begins to pant. This is a trick, not being able to open her mouth. *Why can't I open my mouth? Am I going to suffocate? I can only breathe through my nose. What if my nose gets clogged?* Her breathing progresses into hyperventilating. She begins getting dizzy.

Wait a minute. I'm hyperventilating. Why? That isn't going to help anything. I have to slow my breathing. I can do that. I've done it before. It's just a case of mind over matter.

With a conscious effort, Paige begins a breathing exercise. Four counts in, three counts out. Four counts in, three counts out. She gets control over her breathing.

Okay, now what? Take inventory. Start at my toes, and work my way up. First of all, my feet. Can't move them ... but I can feel them. Can I move my toes? Yes.

Ankles? Can't feel them. Can't move them. Tied together? Well, secured somehow.

Legs, torso ... HAVE I BEEN RAPED? No. Don't think so.

Arms. Can't move them. They're in front of me, and I can feel them, but they won't move. My wrists? Are they tied? Or taped? Or metal handcuffs? Trying to turn my wrist feels sticky instead of prickly. Must be tape, not rope.

Okay, if I can assume they used tape, then that's probably what's over my mouth and eyes. They taped them shut.

Wait! They who? No, wait, keep inventorying.

Even though I'm taped up like a Christmas present, they still have a bag or pillow case or something over my head. No, can't be a pillow case. Smells slightly of fish and cigarettes.

Okay, inventory done; what am I lying on? Can't be a bed. Or a couch. It's too uncomfortable. I guess it's either a cot or a bunk.

And it's moving. With a slight rolling motion. I can hear a deep rumble of a diesel engine. I'm on a boat!

But why? And who? Is this a joke of some sort? I don't know anyone sick enough to do this for a joke.

All of these thoughts are calming, and Paige is no longer hyperventilating. She's not calm. She knows she's in trouble. But at least now her mind is back in control.

She didn't know how long she had been unconscious, and didn't know how long she had lain there since waking. Now that she had inventoried her physical body it was time to consider her situation. *But what do I have to go on? How can I think about what is happening or what to do when I simply have no idea at all what's happening?*

After an unknown length of time, Paige heard a metal door clang open startling her. "You're awake," rasped a gravelly voice. Paige lay silently, not responding. Heavy footsteps approached. "Why did you ignore our note?"

Note? What note? The warning? With her mouth taped shut all Paige could answer was a muffled, "Mmmph?"

"It was simple enough," the voice said. "You were warned to let it go. You stupid or something?"

"Mmmph." *You idiot. Untape my mouth and I'll tell you who's the stupid one.*

"A big investigation. It was just an old skeleton. No one's been reported missing. No harm's done." He snorted. "Well, except for the guy who died. Why couldn't you just let it go at that?"

So that's what all this was about. But why? What was the big deal?

"The sheriff's office doesn't seem to care. The local police don't care. Why did you have to keep sticking your nose in where it wasn't wanted?"

Paige wasn't sure what was going on. Who had her? What did they want?

"And then you had to get the FBI involved."

"Mmmph?"

"Yeah, you did. The feds don't have anything to do with this. But you had to get them involved. Now what am I going to do with you?"

You could always just let me go and we could forget about this whole thing, Paige thought. She didn't think that was going to happen.

"I don't like the thought of eliminating women," said the voice.

Right. Let's go with that concept, thought Paige. *I like that way of thinking.*

"But you've caused a lot of trouble for the company and the boss. He is truly pissed."

Who? thought Paige. *Who's pissed? What company? What does a company have to do with the skeleton? Dang it, what's going on?*

"So the boss, he told me to take care of you. Too bad, you're a good-looking woman."

Paige stiffened.

"No, ain't nobody gonna mess with you like that. Still, I don't think you'll much like what we are gonna do." He paused for a moment. "Or maybe you will. You gotta good sense of humor?"

Laughing he left the room and the door clanged shut loudly behind him.

Paige was angry. Not just with being snatched. She was furious that they wouldn't even untape her mouth long enough for her to try to talk her way out of this. Or, barring that, to tell them in no uncertain terms just what she thought of this whole thing.

About an hour later Paige heard the rumble of the diesel engine lessen and felt the rolling of the boat increase. She knew little about boats, so she didn't realize this meant that they had stopped steaming and hove to, giving the waves more play with the hull. *Now what?* she wondered.

The door clanged open again. This time she heard several sets of boots walking to where she lay. "Okay, get her up," said the gravelly voice, and she was lifted by two people, one at her head and another at her feet. "Let's go."

The men carried Paige none too gently. It felt like they had left the room she had been in, traveled down a passageway, up a companionway, and through a hatch onto the weather deck of a boat.

Must be night, thought Paige. *I don't feel any sun and the breeze is right fresh.*

Paige felt herself being eased over the rail. *They're not going to throw me overboard, are they?*

Unceremoniously she was dropped into the bottom of a dinghy moored next to the boat. Her stiff muscles screamed in pain. With her mouth taped shut she couldn't tell the men what she thought of their handling.

"Let's go," said gravel voice.

The small motor started on the dinghy and they ran for only fifteen minutes before bumping against something. "Be careful, there," said gravel voice. "Get those bumpers over."

Paige lay there as they apparently moored the dinghy to whatever they had run into.

"Bring her," said gravel voice. One of the men lifted her to a standing position and passed her to the other man standing above them and about two feet away.

Paige still wasn't allowed to walk, with her ankles taped together, so the two men picked her up again.

Where on earth am I? she wondered. *Am I on land? Are they going to abandon me on Gilligan's Island?*

The men dropped Paige and what she landed on wasn't sand or dirt. It didn't seem to be the steel of a deck, either. Then the smell of guano hit her, and she knew.

"You'll get a kick out of this girl," said gravel voice. "You're back on board that concrete ship at the breakwater, the Thacher.

We're gonna leave you in a place you're real familiar with—right where you found the last skeleton."

They pushed Paige under something—probably the overhanging superstructure and tied her taped hands over her head. "Don't want you to kick around and bruise yourself," said gravel voice, and they tied her feet to another stationary object..

"How's that?" asked gravel voice. "You good and secure?"

As if in answer to his question Paige struggled violently against her bonds. All to no avail.

Laughing gravel voice said, "Wonder how long it'll take for you to become a skeleton, a scrawny little female skeleton," and he left Paige alone on the deck of the concrete ship of the Kiptopeke Breakwater.

Chapter Fifteen

WEDNESDAY

HURRICANE DARRELL, STEERED by a high-pressure system moving in from the Midwest, had turned east out to sea. It would not hit the Eastern Shore. There would be rain bands and occasional gales of wind. And the high-pressure system was bringing cooler weather with it. So for the most part the weather over the Eastern Shore was looking reasonably pleasant. If you could get in out of the rain.

Paige could not. She was still trussed up partially lying under the superstructure of the ship. At first the drops of rain felt good.

Her head now uncovered, but in just a bra and panties Paige had baked in the hot sun during the day. Her skin was burned and her thirst was raging. She couldn't catch any of the rainwater in her mouth—her head and upper torso were shoved under the overhang. Paige had prayed for relief from the hot sun. Now her prayers were being answered. She'd have to remember to be more careful what she prayed for.

During the sunny periods Paige had been afraid she'd die of dehydration or heatstroke. Now she wondered if hypothermia would finally claim her. *Maybe hypothermia wouldn't be so bad,* she thought. *Just drifting off to sleep and not waking up again.* With this thought, she lapsed into a coma-like sleep.

MEANWHILE DONNA WAS becoming more and more perturbed. She called Pam, but the postmistress still hadn't heard anything. She tried Paige's brother Billy, at the funeral home, but he was just surly. He wasn't worried about Paige. It was his considered opinion that she had gone off just to spite him and make him come in off his fishing boat and do some work. Donna came close to slamming the phone down on his whining.

She went to see Sergeant Heath at the Cape Charles Police Department.

"Has she been gone for over twenty-four hours?" he asked.

"Yes," replied Donna, fudging a bit on the time-line.

"Did she disappear from Cape Charles?"

Ooops. This was going to cause some trouble. "Well, we aren't sure," she said.

"Miss Donna, you know Paige don't live in Cape Charles. And you know she don't work here neither. Now, where was she when she went missing?"

"Sergeant, isn't that kind of the definition of 'missing'—you don't know where she is? Or was?"

"In other words, you're trying to involve me in something that is not part of my jurisdiction?"

"Well …"

"Did you go to the sheriff?"

"Yes. He won't do anything until tomorrow."

"Tomorrow? I thought you said she's been gone for twenty-four hours."

"Well, I might have … fudged that some."

"Miss Donna, you're asking me to get involved in a missing persons case where the person hasn't been missing for the requisite twenty-four hours, and where it isn't even in my jurisdiction—? What do you think I can do? Have you checked with Nott? Those two are close, and he stays at her Eastville apartment times, maybe she stayed out with him."

"NOTT!" she exclaimed. "Why on earth didn't I think of him? Thanks, sergeant," she called as she rushed out of his office.

On the sidewalk outside the Cape Charles Police Department, she called her husband, Jim.

"Jim, I need you to get the shallow-draft flats boat and run me up the creek to Nott's."

"What for?" he asked.

"Just meet me at the marina right now. I'm in a hurry." She hung up, got in her car, and drove to Kings Creek Marina to meet Jim.

Together they rode out of Kings Creek and up to Cherrystone Creek. As they approached Nott's shack Donna was relieved to see his scow moored to one of the shack's supporting stilts.

"Thank goodness, he's here," said Donna. "Nott!" she called.

The door to the shack opened and Nott stepped out onto the weathered board walkway that surrounded the shack.

"Yo, Donna," he called. "Jim."

Donna reached out and grabbed one of the salt-encrusted stilts well above the line of barnacles and held them in place while Jim shut down the motor.

"Nott, is Paige out here with you?"

"Huh? Why would she be out here?"

"She's missing and we are looking everywhere. You haven't heard from her?"

"Donna, you know I ain't got no phone. No, how long's she been gone?"

"Only about a day, but she's not at work nor at her apartment. Her car's at her apartment. So's Pongo, her cat. But there's no sign of her."

"Have you called Tim Hannegan?" asked Nott.

"Yes," replied Donna. "He's coming over, I think sometime today. Maybe he can help."

As Jim and Donna prepared to leave, Nott said, "Now listen: let me know if there's anything I can do."

"Sure will," said Donna. She thought for a minute. "Nott, you ever think about getting one of those disposable cell phones? Just for emergencies?" Unspoken were the words, *like this one*.

"Naw, I ain't. But I guess maybe I oughta." He waved, and they pulled away heading back to the marina.

When they were moored at the marina, Donna said to Jim, "I just don't know how he lives with no electricity, no running water, and no phone."

Jim, the pragmatic sportsman, replied, "A worry-free life," and shook his head appreciatively.

It was early evening when Tim Hannegan called Donna. "I just got off the Bridge-Tunnel. The winds from that storm ... I was afraid they were going to close it up before I got over. They weren't letting trucks or campers on. Anyway, I thought maybe I'd check in at the Cape Charles Hotel. Or the B&Bs."

"I could give you the key to Paige's place."

"No, until we've got a better handle on what's happening I'm going to consider her apartment a crime scene."

Donna gasped. "You think something bad's happened to her?"

"Donna, I don't know. But one thing I know is to always take care not to mess up anything that might ultimately prove useful. If you can give me the key tomorrow, I'll go over and take a look."

"You know where it is?"

"Oh," said Tim sounding somewhat guilty. "Yeah. I've been there. Just dropping her off after dinner."

"Oh. Yeah. Well, I'll meet you at the Cape Charles Coffee House for breakfast. Eight work for you?"

"Certainly."

THURSDAY

ACTUALLY TIM WAS up at five the next morning. He put on his running gear and went for a run. He wasn't a competitive runner, but he loved to run in new areas he visited to sightsee. Cape Charles was laid out in a square grid and wasn't very large, so he crisscrossed back and forth until he had covered the whole town. He passed Haley Goffigon Smith jogging downtown with a friendly wave and ended up on the beach where he forced himself to do sprints through the soft sand while the sun came up in the east. He ended up walking out on the pier where he and Paige had eaten their ice cream cones. He thought of how they had held hands watching the sunset. *Where are you, girl?* He worried. *If anyone has hurt you ... there'll be hell to pay from me.* He then slowly walked back to the hotel while he cooled down.

He showered and dressed down in khaki Dockers, Sperry boat shoes, and a dark blue golf shirt with the FBI seal embroidered on the pocket. Then he walked to the Coffee House.

Donna was waiting for him at a small table on the left back close to the coffee bar and case displaying the fresh pastries. She was already sipping a coffee and waved to Roberta to bring one for Tim.

As they sipped their coffee and nibbled on croissants Donna gave the key to Paige's apartment to Tim. "Tim, please feed and water Pongo while you're in there, okay?"

"Of course. Donna, I think I'll take my stuff and stay there until we finally have some resolution on this. I'll sleep on her couch, as long as I don't find any evidence. I've put in for some vacation days so I can stay here and help find Paige."

Chapter Sixteen

PONGO WASN'T CERTAIN about this new human. He'd smelled him before, on his old human, the woman, but that didn't mean he trusted him. Growling he retreated down the hallway.

Tim stood in the doorway of Paige's apartment. He closely examined the front door lock and where the deadbolt slid into the door frame. There were scratches in the metal of the lock. That could mean that the lock had been picked, or it could mean that Paige at some time had trouble getting the key into the lock. Perhaps after too much partying. The door frame was fine. No sign of a forcible entry.

He silently looked around without going in and just listened. He thought of this as letting the scene "talk" to him. The drapes were open to the view of the Chesapeake. All the furniture was apparently in their normal locations—at least he didn't see any signs on the floor of it having been moved. The smell ... well, there was the stink of an over-ripe litter box, but here, in the entry, there was no whiff of the tang of cordite from a recently fired gun or the coppery smell of blood. Thank the Lord for that. The pictures on the wall hung straight. No obvious spots where any were missing. Magazines lay on the coffee table, neatly stacked.

He stepped inside and closed the door behind him. It snicked shut smoothly. No out-of-alignment from force. Again he just stood, looked around and listened. Nothing new.

He entered the kitchen. Whew! There was the litter box over in the corner. And now Pongo had decided that even if he wasn't going to trust this new human, he'd design to allow Tim to feed him. He mewed loudly and forcibly rubbed up against Tim's leg. When an eighteen pound Maine Coon cat wants your attention, he can usually get it. His rub up against Tim was not kitten-ish. It was more like being hit by a high school middle linebacker.

"Okay," said Tim. "I get the idea. You want to be fed. Chill out. Let me examine the kitchen first."

Before rummaging through the cabinets looking for Pongo's food, Tim carefully examined the kitchen from his place in the doorway. Dirty dishes sat in the sink, but only from about a single meal. Knife block with one empty slot ... oh, there it is, in the sink. Stools pushed up to the breakfast bar. Crumbs on the bar not wiped up. Nothing apparently out of place. Also lying on the counter were two plastic zip-closed bags. One contained a medallion—of Saint Peter, while the other held just a few brown hairs. They were too short to be Paige's, and besides, why would she put her own hair in a plastic bag? He placed the two bags in his pocket.

He went through the cabinets until he found a large can of cat food. Opening it, he took a fork and levered out a glutinous blob of the stinky stuff and put it in the food bowl that was already on the floor. Pongo attacked it as though he hadn't eaten in a week. Tim knew that Donna had fed him the day before, so he wasn't fooled.

He looked through all the cabinets. Nothing. He opened the refrigerator and sniffed the quart of milk. Not sour yet. He put it back. Nothing in the freezer or the oven. Very typical.

Walking down the hallway to Paige's bedroom, Tim took a glance in the powder room. It looked untouched, ready for company.

Paige's bedroom, though, was kind of a mess. He again stood in the doorway and looked and let the room speak to him. In spite of the seriousness of the situation he almost had to laugh. In this case it spoke to him of a single girl not expecting any visitors. Clothes were tossed on the floor and a chair. Through the open door he spotted a towel, presumably wet, tossed over the shower curtain rod in the *en suite* bathroom. The bed was unmade, but ... *wait a minute*, it looked as though there had been a brief struggle. The sheets didn't just look slept in, they were pulled from the bed onto the floor. And there was no blanket or coverlet or duvet.

And there was a smell. Over the sweet expected aroma of young woman, there was something else. Following his nose Tim went to the bedside trashcan and retrieved a white rag that had been thrown there. Waving it gently before his nose he caught a sweet chemical smell that he recognized—chloroform.

Quickly Tim left the apartment making certain the door was secured. He took out his phone and called the Northampton County Sheriff's Department.

"This is Tim Hannegan with the FBI. I am at the apartment of Paige Reese on Wilkins Beach, and I want to report a probable abduction. I need a detective and a crime scene team over here immediately."

The deputy who had answered the phone sounded a bit confused by the rapid-fire orders. "You need what? You want to report a missing person?"

"I said that there has been a probable abduction. I need your people to secure the crime scene and process it for evidence."

"And who did you say you were?"

Beginning to fume Tim replied, "This is Special Agent Timothy Hannegan of the Federal Bureau of Investigation. I am at the apartment of one Paige Reese whom, I understand, has already been reported to you as missing. My initial look in her apartment has revealed irregularities that your department needs to investigate. So you need to get a detective and a crime scene team over here to protect the site. Now! Understand?"

"Well, what's the FBI doing involved in this?"

Infuriated Tim spoke much more slowly and quietly. "Young man, if you don't get someone over here in the next ten minutes I will have the Director of the Federal Bureau of Investigation personally call your sheriff to report your flaming incompetence. Got it?"

About fifteen minutes later the apartment had been secured with crime scene tape and a seemingly professional team of investigators was going through it inch-by-inch looking for evidence. They had bagged the chloroform rag, but as of yet, they had found nothing else useful.

"And you were here why, Special Agent?" asked sheriff's detective Si Brooks.

"As I said, detective, Miss Reese and I are friends. When she went missing, and her local friends were unable to locate her or, apparently, get anything going professionally, they called me to see if she happened to be with me."

Si nodded, meticulously taking notes in a little spiral-topped notebook. He was of an indeterminate middle-age, dumpy, frumpy, and wearing a sport coat about seventeen years out-of-date. The tip of his tongue protruded from the side of his mouth as he concentrated on his note-taking. Tim was less-than impressed.

"So they were making a kidnapping report to the Bureau?"

"No, detective. Can I call you Si? You call me Tim. That'll make it easier. No, Si, Paige and I had worked together on something a while ago, but since then it has been more of a personal relationship."

"You sleeping with her ... uh, Tim?"

"Not that that is any of your concern, but no! Right now it's just a new relationship. But we are very fond of each other."

"Fond—"

"Oh, come on! Quit trying to make something where nothing exists. We're friends. Without privileges. Will it progress to something beyond that? I hope so. Right now, that's where it is." Tim ran a hand through his hair.

"Her friends called me not because I'm with the Bureau, but because they know we are fond of each other, and they think of me as just a law enforcement officer. I guess they hoped that our personal relationship would spur me on when your department was still waiting for protocols to allow you to take it as a missing persons case.

"So I came over, I met with her best friend Donna Bozza, who gave me a key, and I came over to make a preliminary go through. When I found the chloroform rag I immediately backed out and called for you. It's your jurisdiction. I don't want to step on any toes or get in the way."

"Uh, huh," muttered Brooks as he ducked under the crime scene tape and back into the apartment.

Chapter Seventeen

FRIDAY MORNING

PAIGE HAD STOPPED shivering. It wasn't just because the sun was out, which it was. Paige knew enough about how a body reacts to heat-sapping cold and wet to know that she was slipping into hypothermia. *It's not so bad,* she thought. *Just go to sleep and that's it. Watermen who fall overboard and don't drown often die from hypothermia. It's painless. I can't feel my hands or toes already. My legs feel like waterlogged timbers. Just let it go, Paige. Let go and sleep. So tired.* Again she drifted off. Paige's core body temperature had dropped to 94.7 degrees.

TIM DROVE TO the sheriff's office and sat in one of the uncomfortable plastic-and-metal chairs in the lobby waiting for Detective Brooks to finish at Paige's apartment and return to his office. When Brooks came in and saw Tim sitting there he gave him a look of frustrated disgust before waving him back to his office.

Tim thought the office looked like Brooks. Everything on the desk was perfectly lined up in parallel. There were no loose papers about nor empty coffee cups sitting around. The bank calendar hanging on the wall had each day carefully crossed out with a black sharpie. Tim would be willing to swear that it had been done with a ruler.

It was obvious that Brooks didn't like Tim, and he didn't like the FBI, or any other agency, looking over his shoulder while he worked. It wasn't insecurity, it was just that he was certain that when the FBI came in they would bogart the investigation.

"Okay," said Brooks, "what can I do for you?"

"Si, I was hoping that I might be of some help to you. I've worked some major abduction cases, and I thought you might appreciate a different set of eyes looking at this one."

"Special Agent ..."

"Tim."

"Right. Tim. We might be just a little sheriff's office in a rural county, but ... well, we've got telephones and computers and all sorts of fancy equipment."

"Whoa, Si. I wasn't trying to cast aspersions. I just have some experience and wanted to offer it."

"Well ... *Tim* ... I do appreciate that. But we've got protocols to follow, and they usually do us real good for solving things like this."

"You mind if I ask what you are going to do?" asked Tim.

"Well, we just follow a logical progression. That's how to solve most anything—follow the logic." Brooks leaned back in his office chair, which did not dare squeek, and laced his hand behind his head before pedantically continuing.

"First we got to make sure someone really is missing. You know how many times we get missing persons reports that are bogus? Guy gets in a fight with his wife, or wife forgets to tell husband that she's going up to Salisbury shopping. Next thing you know they're calling us to make a report. So we got to make sure that it's for real."

"You know this is for real. We found the rag with the chloroform."

"Maybe. Maybe not. Then we got to talk to friends and family to see the vic's mental state."

"Vic?"

"Victim. Have they been depressed or sick or anything? Talk with their doctor and see what he has to say." Brooks leaned forward in his chair and straightened a paperweight shaped like a sheriff's badge that must have been millimetrically out-of-place.

"We got to look around their home and see if anything looks amiss there. Is there any luggage missing? Are their toiletries still in the bathroom? Has the fridge been cleared out? You know, stuff like that."

"Detective, her keys were left in her apartment. Her car was parked in the parking lot. Her cat was left alone with no extra food or water. Don't you think that's a bit suspicious?"

"Well, sure, but we've got to check off all of the boxes as we go to make sure we don't overlook something important. As a law enforcement professional yourself, you know how important it is to be thorough."

Tim nodded his head, resignedly. Going through their protocol point-by-point was going to be painfully slow, and if Paige was in trouble she might not have that much time.

"Then we have to check with the Virginia State Police as well as the Shore Regional Hospital and any emergency clinics in the area. You know in case she was hurt or took sick all of a sudden. We'll check with the ambulance squads, too."

By now Tim knew he was wasting his time talking with Detective Brooks. Their protocol might be fine for a run-of-the-mill case, but this case was emergent. He just knew it. Paige's vanishing was not a simple illness or argument. She'd been forcibly taken, by person or persons unknown, and time was of the essence in finding her.

Brooks droned on about their protocols and checklists while Tim got increasingly perturbed.

"Listen, Si," he finally said, "that sounds like a great plan. You go with it. Just please let me know if any ransom demand shows up."

"Sure, Tim," replied the detective. "I'll be happy to keep you up to speed on what's happening. 'Brotherhood of blue,' and such."

Tim held back a retching laugh as he exited the office. Outside he called Donna and asked for a meeting. She was at her office in Eastville, so in less than five minutes he was sitting opposite her desk.

"We've got a problem," Tim said without preamble. "I'm sure the protocols and S.O.P.s Brooks follows are well thought out and competent, but I don't think we've got time for him to go through them. I think Paige is in physical trouble, and we need to act now."

"Has anyone heard from whoever took her?" asked Donna.

"No," said Tim, "and that's one of the things that bothers me the most. If it were kidnappers looking for money, we should have heard *something* by now. I know this is silly, but if it were *terrorists*, they would have said something. If it were an accident, we would have *found* something. But to be this totally clueless … that worries me."

"What can we do?" asked Donna.

"The sheriff's department is going to cross all the T's and dot all the I's of the checklist stuff. Let's us do stuff out of the norm."

"Like what?"

"That gallery of aerial photography that's near the coffee house in Cape Charles, 'At Altitude'? Does he live around here?"

"The photographic artist Gordon Campbell. Yes. He flies his light sport aircraft from Campbell Field Airport up in Weirwood."

"Where?"

"It's a little community just up the highway."

Tim asked, "Do you think he might do some aerial reconnaissance for us?"

"I'm sure he would," replied Donna. "Gordon loves to fly and he loves to help out. He lives down in Cape Charles. I'll give him a call."

THE WEATHER WAS continuing to hold, Hurricane Darrell having dissipated over the colder waters of the mid-Atlantic, and the little red Dragonfly raced along at almost 40 knots, or almost 46 miles per hour. It wasn't fast, but it made for a much more thorough search. The main problem was that the Rotax 912S engine was going to suck through the six gallons of gasoline pretty quickly with both Gordon, the pilot, and Donna on board. But it couldn't be helped. Donna insisted that she go as another set of eyes, and that was it.

The most difficult place to search was going to be the bayside of The Shore, so that was where they started, initially flying down to Mallard Cove Marina and working north from there.

There were a lot of people enjoying the beach and sandbar at The Jackspot, but their distress was going to come tomorrow morning when the hangovers attacked.

This was the first time Donna had flown over the area in the Dragonfly, and she loved it. Even though she was a "come here," she adored The Shore, and seeing it from this new perspective just reinforced that love. She hoped Jim would be out at their Mermaid Bay Beach home when she flew over.

They flew the beach north until they reached Kiptopeke State Park. Donna hadn't lived on The Shore when the ferry was still docking here, but she'd been to the park often and even kayaked out around the breakwater of sunken concrete World War II liberty ships. She had never boarded any of them, so she asked the pilot to fly low over the ships so that she could see what they looked like from above. It wasn't much. They'd been sitting there on the bottom since 1948, subject to The Bay and the weather. The pelicans didn't seem to mind how decrepit they were. *I imagine they love a stable platform to work from when they are fishing. And I know that these hulks do attract the fish. I remember the huge rockfish Jim caught out here—*

"Wait a minute!" she cried out. "Gordon, circle back. I saw something. QUICK! CIRCLE BACK!"

The Dragonfly circled and throttled back to near its 25-knot stall speed while it dropped almost onto the deck of the ship. "There! Do you see it? There! Legs! Sticking out from under that overhang. That's got to be her. It's got to."

Despite the noise from the Dragonfly's engine Donna got on her cell phone and dialed Tim. Sticking her finger in one ear as best she could, and listening hard she yelled, "Tim! I think we found her! On the same ship where they found that skeleton. All I could see was legs sticking out, but it's got to be her."

Tim tried to answer and ask some questions, but there was too much noise on Donna's end.

"Get a boat and get out there now. Call the Coast Guard. Call Jim. Call everybody, but get out there now." Donna disconnected. She looked over at Gordon and motioned north, back to his airfield. They'd done it.

Chapter Eighteen

LATE FRIDAY AFTERNOON

FORTUNATELY IT HADN'T rained that night, and the weather stayed balmy. Paige's clothing had dried out. In fact, she was not even sweaty as Paige was now suffering dehydration as well as hypothermia. She remained unconscious. Her core body temperature was now 93.2 degrees.

WORRIED BUT IN control Tim called the Coast Guard at Station Cape Charles and alerted them to the situation. They said that they would immediately scramble one of their rigid hull inflatable (RHIB) patrol boats to the Kiptopeke Breakwater. They also would contact Coast Guard Air Station Elizabeth City and see if there were any Coast Guard helicopters operating in the area.

Satisfied he had done all he could Tim jumped in his car and raced south down the highway to Kiptopeke State Park. Flashing his credentials at the guard at the entrance, he hardly slowed until he reached the water.

As he jumped from his car he spotted two Coast Guardsmen aboard the concrete ship. Racing to the water's edge he again used his FBI credentials to commandeer a young woman's kayak and paddle himself out to the ship. He carefully made his way to where the Coast Guardsmen knelt working on a supine figure. It looked as though one of them was performing CPR.

CLIMBING UP ON the hulk Tim badged the Coast Guardsmen. "How is she?"

"When we reached her body we checked for a pulse and breathing. Her lips were blue and her pupils were dilated and non-reactive. But with hypothermia we're trained that a person isn't dead until they are *warm* and dead." They continued working.

The senior man began CPR as his partner wrapped Paige in a reflective emergency blanket. Cutting her hands free from the stanchion he lowered her arms and started an IV of saline solution.

Tim pulled a knife from his pocket and cut her legs loose. Without breaking the rhythm of the CPR they slid her completely out onto the deck.

Tim wanted so badly to do something, but he knew enough to stay out of the way and let the professionals work. He took out his handkerchief, which was wet from his kayaking, and used it to wipe some of the guano that had accumulated on Paige while she was tied up.

The Coast Guardsmen traded off on the CPR, and the senior man took a radio from his belt. Calling his station, he was advised that a Coast Guard HH-65 Dolphin helicopter had been transiting the Chesapeake Bay en route to Air Station Elizabeth City and had been diverted to their location. Waiting for the helicopter he now helped his partner with the CPR, performing the compressions while the other man did the breathing.

Tim heard the distinctive whistling whop-whop of a Coast Guard Dolphin, and looked out over The Bay. Coming in from the northeast he could see the helicopter in the livery of the Coast Guard. *Hurry up*, he thought. *I don't want to lose her.* He smoothed the hair back from Paige's forehead and gave her an air-kiss. "Hang in there, cowgirl. We've got a lot of stuff left to do."

Coast Guard Dolphins have an autopilot function that brings the helicopter into a stable hover at fifty-feet. The side door slid open, and a rescue swimmer was lowered down to the deck with a Stokes basket. Unclipping from his harness he carried the Stokes litter over to where the other two men were still performing CPR. Reaching into his satchel he produced an Ambu bag. Placing the mask over Paige's mouth and nose he began to squeeze the bag to help her breathe.

"Check for a pulse," he directed.

The Coast Guardsman who had been doing the chest compressions placed two fingers on the side of Paige's throat. "Got it. Weak and thready, but it's there."

They secured Paige in the Stokes basket, and the rescue swimmer rode up with her to keep squeezing the Ambu bag. One of the crewmen on board the helicopter pulled them in, and before the door had completely slid closed they were racing north up The Bay.

"Where are they taking her?" asked Tim.

"The closest civilian hospital is Shore Memorial up in Onancock. They'll take her up there."

"Great. Guys, thank you so much. You've saved her life."

The two Coast Guardsmen shyly acknowledged Tim's praise. "That's what they pay us the big bucks for," said the senior man.

As they began to clean up their equipment Tim returned to his borrowed kayak and returned to shore.

"Wow, that was something!" said the young woman with the kayak. "What happened?"

"Sorry," said Tim. "I've really got to get going. Maybe it'll be in tomorrow's paper." He ran to his car and raced back up the highway toward the hospital in Onancock.

He telephoned Donna on his way north and told her what was happening. She said that she'd meet him at the hospital.

By the time he reached the hospital the helicopter had already left the helipad. Although his thoughts were centered on Paige, he was still sorry that he hadn't had the chance to thank the crew of the Dolphin. He made a mental note to himself to track them down and buy them a case of beer. Better send a case to Coast Guard Station Cape Charles, too.

Tim rushed into the emergency room. Donna was sitting off to the side in the waiting area. She jumped up and ran to Tim. "They won't let me in. They won't tell me anything," she lamented.

"Okay. Wait here," said Tim as he walked to the admitting desk. "I'd like to know about Paige Reese. She just came in on a Coast Guard helicopter."

"Are you a relative?" asked the nurse, a pinch-faced woman in her sixties with a disapproving glare.

"No, but—"

"Sorry, but I can't give you any information."

"I understand that, nurse, but — "

"Sir, if you are not family, I cannot give you any information." She turned and started walking away.

Tim yanked his badge case from his pocket, flipped it open, and said, "Ma'am, I'd like to speak with your supervisor. Now!"

The nurse turned back, ready for a fight. Then she saw the badge. "You're ... police?"

"FBI."

"Uh, yessir," she said subdued. "Just a moment. I'll get her doctor."

She came back out with a young man who was dressed in blue jeans and a green scrub shirt. She pointed the doctor in Tim's direction then returned to her station behind the desk.

"Hey," said the doctor. "You wanted to know about Paige Reese?"

"Just a minute," said Tim, and he waved Donna over to join them.

"Uh, yes," he said.

"Is she involved in a Bureau investigation?" asked the doctor. "You know about the Federal HIPPA laws, protect a patient's privacy."

Tim kind of finessed the answer. "Well, she was just rescued from being abducted," he said, intimating that it was being investigated by the FBI.

"Oh, well then," said the doctor, "you know she was suffering from severe hypothermia when they brought her in. Her core temperature was just over 91 degrees. It's supposed to be 98.6. At that temperature her internal organs, like her liver and heart begin to shut down to provide more blood to the brain. That's why when she came in they were breathing for her with an Ambu bag."

"Okay, but how is she now?"

The doctor continued, "She was somewhat comatose, which is normal with this degree of hypothermia. You know, the body tries to protect itself. It's really remarkable how—"

"Doctor", interrupted Tim. "How is she now?"

"Oh, yes, well, she was also quite dehydrated. That too can cause organs to fail and the body to shut down. No one ever told me how she came to be in this state."

Frustrated, Tim said, "She was abducted in her pajamas and tied outside, unprotected, in the sun and rain for several days. Now, doctor, I ask you *again*, HOW IS SHE NOW?"

"Oh, yes, I'm sorry," the doctor stammered. "She's fine. She's receiving warmed IV fluids, and she is nestled under warmed blankets. She has one of those heat bags, you know the ones that warm up chemically? She has one of those in each armpit."

"She'll be all right?"

"Oh, yes. I've got a sedative in her drip right now, so she'll sleep until at least tomorrow. But barring anything untoward, she should make a full recovery and be discharged … oh, probably late tomorrow."

He'd finally gotten the information he wanted.

"Can we see her?"

"No," said the doctor. "I don't want her disturbed. And you won't be able to communicate with her, anyway. Come back in the morning."

Tim's relief was palpable. He wasn't the crying-type, but he was shaken to his core. Taking Donna by the arm Tim walked out of the hospital. Paige was all right. Now it was time to figure out who was responsible.

Chapter Nineteen

SATURDAY

PAIGE SLOWLY SWAM her way up toward the light. *Am I dead?* she wondered. *Is this that light they say you see at the end of the tunnel?* She felt warm and comfortable. *If I'm dead, at least I'm not hot. This can't be hell.* Her mind drifted as did her body. Now she could hear people. Were they calling to her? *Are those the angels calling me to heaven?* she wondered? *Not very musical if they are. Kind of disappointing.*

Someone was definitely calling her name, but from a great distance. "Paige? Paige? Can you hear me, Paige?" She thought to herself, *yeah I can hear you. Why don't you just leave me alone? I'm comfortable here.*

"Paige, if you can hear me, open your eyes. Come on, girl, open your eyes."

Why would I want to do that? That light's awful bright out there.

There was a loud CRACK of sharply clapped hands. "PAIGE! Open your eyes!"

Slowly Paige forced her eyes to flutter open. When she did the bright light wasn't there. Instead, right in front of her, almost nose-to-nose, were the most beautiful turquoise-blue eyes. She blinked.

"Okay, Paige," said Tim Hannegan. "Welcome back to the land of the living. We almost lost you there."

Paige was confused. *Lost me where? And where am I now?* She struggled to sit up. Tim slid an arm under her shoulders and lifted her just enough to place another pillow under her head.

In a rusty voice, Paige said, "Where am I?"

From behind Tim, Donna chimed in. "You're in the hospital in Onancock. Do you remember anything about the past few days?"

Whispering she replied, "I remember being cold. So very cold." She closed her eyes again.

Tim took her hand and squeezed it. Weakly she squeezed back, and then she was gone, back to sleep.

Tim walked out into the hallway and down to the nurse's station. "Is Paige's doctor available?"

They sat in a staff lounge down the hall from Paige's room. "She woke up for a few minutes and recognized me," said Tim. "That's good, right?"

"Of course it is," replied the doctor. "She's young and strong. Apparently her exposure wasn't too long; she'll be fine."

"When can she go home?"

"Uh, well ..." The doctor started equivocating. "You know, her well-being is foremost, and we will want to make absolutely sure—"

Tim interrupted. "Doc, I don't want to do anything that will harm her. But she was just kidnapped and left to die out in the weather. I not only want to make sure that she is well, but I have to make sure that she is safe, and I have to find out what the heck happened." Tim's words were heated, and the doctor was nodding his head. "Now, I ask you again, when can she go home?"

"Yes, well, considering all that," said the doctor, "and if she continues to improve, I'm sure that she will be able to be discharged sometime tomorrow.

Should I arrange for hospital security to watch over her?"

"No," said Tim. "I'll be here until you release her."

Sunday

Early the next morning, well before the dawn, the nursing assistant came in to get Paige's vital signs. The squeezing of the blood pressure cuff woke Paige and when she saw her the nurse pointed to the corner.

Tim was there, asleep in the recliner.

"Has he been there all night?" whispered Paige.

The nurse smiled, nodding her head.

How about that? Thought Paige to herself. *That's sweet.*

She motioned to the nurse to help her out of bed, and she went to the bathroom to pee. Coming out she eased over to the sink where she brushed her teeth, washed her face, and brushed her hair. She wanted to be presentable for Tim when he awoke. Turning to go back to the bed she saw that Tim was awake, watching her, with a strange smile on his face.

Omigosh, the hospital gown! She crab-walked sideways back to the bed while Tim laughed loudly.

"How long have you been awake?" she demanded.

"Oh, since the girl came in to take your vitals," he replied, smiling.

"And you didn't say anything?"

"No, I didn't know if you'd try to go back to sleep, and then the show … well, it was too cute to spoil."

Paige felt the red start at her chest and quickly climb to the top of her head. "That has got to be the most inconsiderate and underhanded and rude thing I have ever heard of. Why, if my daddy were still alive he'd thrash you within an inch of your life for taking such liberties. Who do you think you are? WHO DO YOU THINK *I* AM? And what are you doing in my room at this hour of the night? Do you get off watching women sleep, or something? Well? I'm talking to you, Tim Hannegan. Are you going to answer me or just sit there with that stupid look on your face?"

"Ya through?" asked Tim.

"AM I THROUGH? I'll tell you when I'm …" She ran out of steam and flounced back on the bed.

"Well," said Tim. "Along with the hospital gown, that's another side of you I've never seen."

"The hospital gown?" she shouted. As she took a deep breath ready to take off again, Tim put his hand on her shoulder. His touch was electric.

"Calm down, Paige. First of all, we're both adults. Second of all, it's not like I've never seen one of those before."

That started her sitting up again.

"And," he laughed, "as far as those go, it certainly is a nice one." He caught her wrist as she spun to give him a slap across the face. Standing and leaning over the bed he pulled her to him, and kissed her gently on the lips, holding the kiss for what seemed like forever.

When he finally pulled back Paige was breathing so hard she had trouble speaking. "I … you … that was … whew!"

"Yeah," said Tim. "I thought so, too."

As much as Tim wanted to grill her about the abduction, he wanted to respect her physical condition. They sat and chatted about mostly inconsequential things until finally her doctor returned in the middle of the afternoon.

"Miss Reese, how do you feel?"

"I feel like I want to get out of here. Can I go home now?"

"You're certain you don't feel any side effects from your … ordeal?"

"None. I just want to go home."

"Okay, then. Will this gentleman be driving you home?"

"Yes."

"Well, then … get out of here!" And that's exactly what they did.

Chapter Twenty

THEY PULLED OUT of the hospital's parking lot. Tim thought Paige looked cute in the black scrubs the hospital had loaned her. When Tim's car reached the highway and started south they simultaneously turned to each other and said, "What happened?"

"You go first," Tim said.

"I don't know," said Paige. "I have some flashes of baking in the sun then shivering at night, but it's just quick impressions. I don't remember much since feeding Pongo and going to bed ... then waking up here staring at you. What day is this?"

"It's Sunday the eleventh," replied Tim. "You've been missing for four days."

"Four days? I just don't remember—"

"You were supposed to have lunch with Donna on Tuesday. When you didn't show up and wouldn't answer your phone, she got worried."

"Donna! Does she know I'm okay?"

"She's the one who found you. She was flying with Gordon Campbell searching and luckily saw your legs."

"Wait a minute," said Paige. "Saw my legs? An air search? Where was I?"

"You really don't remember any of this, do you?" asked Tim.

Paige shook her head.

"You were found on that same concrete breakwater ship, actually in the exact same place, where they found that skeleton."

"What!?"

"If Gordon hadn't overflown that particular ship in the breakwater you might well have ended up as a skeleton in the same place!"

Paige shivered uncontrollably as a frightened chill quickly swept up her spine.

"Are you certain you don't remember anything?" asked Tim.

"Let's get home to my apartment," said Paige in a wavering voice. "Maybe once I'm there things will come back to me. Right now, I'm still processing waking up in the hospital with you hovering over me like a blue-eyed gargoyle."

"Fair enough, though we'll talk about that 'gargoyle' comment later."

When they walked into Paige's apartment they were startled by an unearthly yowl, and eighteen pounds of Maine Coon cat launched itself from the back of the couch and into Paige's arms, making her stagger.

"Pongo!" she exclaimed. "Did you miss me?"

Pongo wriggled out of her grasp and, muttering and cursing in catish and occasionally glancing back at the two humans, made his way to his empty food bowl in the kitchen. "Yeah, I can see that you did."

After feeding Pongo, and taking a long hot shower, Paige dressed in bluejeans and a bulky Eastern Shore Community College sweatshirt. She poured two glasses of bourbon, and handed one to Tim, then headed for her balcony.

Some time later, Tim and Paige sat in wicker chairs on her balcony overlooking The Bay while Paige tried to free her memory to remember any significant items about her abduction. She did this by performing controlled and programmed deep breathing, a touch of self-hypnosis relaxation, some quiet music playing almost below hearing volume and a generous application of Pappy Van Winkle 20-year old bourbon straight up.

As Paige sat, eyes closed, breathing deeply, Tim watched her closely. When he felt she had reached a relaxed malleable state he leaned in a very quietly said, "Paige."

Paige murmured something, obviously acknowledging him but not wishing to leave her relaxed state.

Tim started softly, almost *sotto voce*. "Paige, don't open your eyes, just hear my voice.

Now listen to your breathing. It's slow and rhythmic, almost as though you were sleeping. Just relax and let your mind wander, but always hear my voice."

Paige took a deep sighing breath and settled more deeply into the cushions of her chair.

Softly, Tim spoke again. "Paige, you are getting more and more relaxed. More and more relaxed. Your muscles are getting so relaxed they feel as though they are just hanging from your bones as you get more and more relaxed. More and more relaxed."

"Do you hear the tinkle of the little wind chimes?" There were no wind chimes, but this was a technique Tim used to test Paige's relaxation and concentration. If she said that she heard no wind chimes, he'd know that she was not yet ready for him to question her. But when asked about hearing the wind chimes, Paige murmured an "Um, hum" in agreement. "Wind chimes."

Tim continued. "Paige I'm going to put my hand on your shoulder and gently press down. As I do so your relaxation will deepen." He did, and Paige let out another long sighing breath. "More and more relaxed. More and more relaxed."

Tim waited a few more moments, allowing Paige's state to deepen. Then he commenced with his questioning.

"Paige, think back to when you were abducted. Visualize it in your mind's eye." He waited a few beats, then asked, "Can you see anything when someone came into your bedroom and took you?"

Almost whispering Paige replied, "No. When I awoke it was all dark."

"Was it night?" asked Tim. "Look around you. Is it night? Do you see any light?"

"No, my eyes are covered. I can't see anything."

"Okay, Paige. Are you blindfolded?"

"It smells!" exclaimed Paige. "I'm not blindfolded. There's a rag being held over my face, and it has a sweetish chemical smell. Everything is getting swimmy and far away. Now my head is in a bag that smells of fish. And cigarettes."

"Okay, Paige. You're doing great. They drugged you with chloroform and you slept. When the chloroform wore off did you cry out when you awoke?"

"My mouth," she said. "My mouth has some sort of tape over it. So do my eyes. My mouth is taped shut! How am I going to breathe?" Paige started hyperventilating. She was deeply under, now, and in her mind these things were actually happening to her in the moment. "I can't breathe! I CAN'T BREATHE!"

Tim quickly moved in. "Paige, your mouth is no longer taped. You have no trouble breathing. Take long slow deep breaths." She did, and calmed quickly. "See? It's okay."

He paused while she calmed down. "Okay," said Tim. "Now, you are awake and breathing fine, but you still have a bag over your head. What do you hear?" He sat quietly waiting.

"I hear … I hear a diesel engine."

"Like a truck or a tractor?"

"No, I feel its vibrations as well as hearing it. And there's movement. Motion. Whatever I'm lying on is rolling slightly. *I'm on a boat!*"

"Good Paige. You're on a boat. What else do you hear or feel?"

Paige sat quietly for a moment. Then she whispered, "Wait a minute. Someone's coming. I can hear their footsteps."

"Is it a man or a woman—can you tell?"

"He's saying something. Oh, what is it? What's he saying? Oh, he's talking about the note. Why didn't I pay attention to their warning note?" She paused, listening.

"Now he's angry that I brought the FBI into it. Why couldn't I just leave well enough alone?"

"What note is that, Paige?"

"The one about leaving the dead rest in peace."

She sat still for a moment before tensing.

"Wait! The boat is stopping. There must be a sea running 'cause it's starting to roll more. I hope I don't puke with this bag over my head.

"Oh! Now they are carrying me off the boat and onto something solid. I'm on my back with my arms stretched over my head. They're tying me to something! 'Please, stop! You're hurting me!'"

Tim moved to Paige's side. "Paige," he said softly. "Paige, listen to me: you're safe. You're in your own apartment. Calm yourself. Breathe deeply. Smell the clean smell of The Bay? Your head isn't covered anymore. Your hand and feet aren't taped. You're fine. You are waking up now. We're sitting on your balcony. I'm going to count to five and with each number, you are going to come more and more awake.

"One. You are waking now. Two. Your eyes are beginning to flutter. Three. Your eyes are opening now and you are feeling very relaxed. Four. Coming more and more awake and remembering everything that happened. Five. You are awake. Go ahead and open your eyes."

Paige's eyes fluttered open, but they were still focused far away.

"Paige!" said Tim commandingly.

Paige turned to him, focused on his face, then threw herself into his arms. "Oh, Tim! I remembered!"

"Maybe a little too much," Tim agreed.

Paige nodded her head. "Yeah, I can see why I blocked all of that.

Tim, who would do that? And why me?"

"I don't know," answered Tim, "but I'm damn well going to find out."

She hadn't seen this deep an anger in Tim before. "Was that hypnosis you just did to me?" Paige asked.

"Well," he answered, "sort of. The courts frown on testimony obtained through hypnosis, but I use some of its techniques to try to develop leads that I can use. Does it bother you?"

"No, it was kind of nice. I was aware of everything that was going on, but I was able to go back to that time, too. And, man, was I relaxed when I woke up." She leaned her head on the back of her chair.

"But I've heard that hypnosis was Satanic ... that the hypnotist takes over the subject's soul."

"I imagine you heard that from the same people who say that Freemasons use babies blood in their rituals. People are always quick to jump at something they don't understand."

"I guess so," she responded. "I think I still have my soul intact."

Tim chuckled.

"Listen," she said, "Do you think you could do that again, and maybe we could dig around and find something in my mind that'll help us track these guys down?"

"Okay, I will," said Tim, "but let's do it tomorrow. After you've had a good night's sleep in your own bed."

"Are you leaving?" asked Paige anxiously. She didn't want to be alone.

"I'm not going back across The Bay," he responded. "Maybe I'll just check in at a bed and breakfast down in Cape Charles."

"You'll do no such thing," she snapped. "I bought this couch because it is big enough and comfortable enough to act as a bed. You go down to your car and get your things, and I'll make it up for you. You'll sleep right here."

Then she looked kind of sheepish. "Besides, I really don't want to be alone tonight."

Chapter Twenty-One

IT WAS ALMOST nine-thirty when Paige awoke the next morning. Tim had turned off her clock-radio alarm and pulled the heavy drapes closed over the windows to help her sleep. He must have closed Pongo out of her room, because he would never have allowed her to sleep this late. He was too demanding.

She got up, performed her morning ablutions, and went out to her living room. Pongo acknowledged her presence loudly, but Tim wasn't there. And she had gone to so much trouble with her makeup to cover the damage to her face caused by her ordeal on the breakwater. Her face wasn't sunburned like much of her lower body. It had been shaded by the overhanging superstructure. But the tape on her eyes and mouth had left angry red marks. At the hospital the doctor had commented about how difficult it had been to remove the "baked on" tape without hurting the underlying tissues. Now she was suffering the result. At least sunglasses and lipstick hid much of the damage.

Paige tried to dress prettily in a pair of skinny jeans and a crisply starched and ironed broadcloth man-cut shirt. But for naught.

She sat on the couch, where the bedding had been neatly folded, and cuddled with Pongo. "Oh, Pongo," she lamented, "do you think I've scared him away?"

Pongo just looked at her with a jaundiced eye and commenced licking his own crotch, his back leg stretched high into the air..

She heard a key in the lock, and looked up as Tim staggered in the door, his arms laden with croissants and cafe con leche from Machipongo Trading Company, cinnamon buns from Kate's Kupboard, a carton of orange juice and another of milk from ShoreStop, a dozen eggs, and a VIRGINIAN PILOT newspaper.

"I was afraid you'd left," she said.

"No. You just didn't have anything decent left in your 'fridge, after being gone so long, so I just picked up some essentials. You don't mind a cafe con leche and croissant, do you?"

"Silly boy," she said as she set the kitchen table with coffee mugs and utensils. "Just hurry up and put that stuff away. I'm famished. They don't feed you real well up at the hospital."

It didn't take them long to devour the coffee and some of the calorie and carb-laden food. Tim washed the dishes and Paige dried and put them away, and then they went back to the living room.

"OKAY," SAID TIM. "You ready to try it again?"

"I'm kind of nervous," said Paige.

"You did real well last night," replied Tim. "But if you don't want to do it, that's fine."

"No, I want to," she said, "but ... well, I've heard about hypnotists that make people do strange things. Like walk around clucking like chickens, and such."

"Paige, those are the guys doing it as a stage act. I use it as a serious investigative tool. Besides, you remember you were aware of everything that was going on. If I start to go someplace you don't want to go, you can refuse. In fact, if you get uncomfortable at any time, you can just wake yourself up. But I promise you I'll not do anything of which you wouldn't approve."

"Well, okay," Paige said. "Should I get out the Pappy Van Winkle bourbon?" She laughed self-consciously.

"No, that was convenient last night, but now that you are aware of what it feels like and what I'm doing, it will be that much easier to get you to relax."

"Oh. Okay. Let's give it a try."

True to his words, it only took about ten minutes for Tim to have Paige completely relaxed and responsive, her eyes comfortably closed.

"Paige?"

"Mmm, hmm?"

"Paige your right arm is getting stiff. There's no pain, but the muscles in your right arm are tightening and your right arm is beginning to rise off your lap. It's beginning to rise …"

Slowly Paige's right arm began to rise and straighten out before her.

"It's rising and getting rigid. It is not disturbing your relaxation, and you are not doing it consciously, it's just as though your right arm has a mind of its own as it is getting rigid, straightening out in front of you. Now, as I press down on your arm it will stay rigid and will resist my pressure. And as I do so you will become more and more relaxed. More and more relaxed."

Tim gently pressed down on Paige's arm while softly saying, "More and more relaxed. More and more relaxed.

"Okay, Paige, your right arm is returning to your lap and the muscles in your right arm are becoming as relaxed as the rest of your body. More and more relaxed."

Tim stopped his patter for a few minutes and just let Paige drift in her relaxed state. Then he said, "Paige, I want you to think back to the night you were abducted. Think back. I want you to go back when you first woke up that night. Can you do that?"

"I was sound asleep. Deep asleep."

"Okay, you are in a deep sleep. What happened next?"

"I … I heard something in the living room. I thought I heard something. I thought maybe Pongo had gotten into something."

"Okay, you are hearing some noise. What are you going to do?"

"Pongo! Are you all right? Don't you go barfing on the couch, you hear me?"

"Then what?"

"I don't know. It's all so foggy and swimmy. I can't remember …"

"What happened next, Paige?" urged Tim quietly.

"Pongo, what's …? There's a soft knock."

"Is it Pongo?"

"No, there's a soft knock at the bedroom door. Maybe it's Tim!"

"What did you do, Paige?"

"I wasn't really awake enough to deal with Tim. Why would Tim be at the bedroom door? I'd better open the door and see …

"YOU'RE NOT TIM! Who are … TIM! Help me, Tim! Wait! What are you doing? What's on that cloth? Why are you pushing me back down on the bed? TIM! Help!"

"EASY, PAIGE. THIS is Tim. I'm here. You're all right."

"Oh, Tim, I saw him! I saw the man who took me. Before he put the rag over my face I saw his face."

By this point Paige was trembling, her breathing quick and ragged.

"Paige, listen to me: the man is no longer here. This is Tim. You are here alone with me. You are safe with me."

Paige's breathing evened out and calmed down.

Kind of interesting that she thought about me while all of this was going down. I'll have to take some time and think about that.

"Paige, you are still very relaxed and you are very safe. You are here in your apartment with just Tim and Pongo. Now, I want you to think back to the man you saw the night you were abducted. I want you to clearly picture him in your mind's eye. Get him clearly and sharply in focus. Concentrate on him. He's not here. He can't hurt you anymore. But I want you to focus on him."

Paige's breathing picked up a little, but she wasn't trembling.

"Do you know him, Paige?"

"No."

"What's he wearing, Paige?"

Softly she spoke. "Canvas pants, a yellow slicker over a brown plaid flannel shirt, white rubber boots, and a ballcap."

"Does the cap have a logo?"

"Omigod, it's filthy! How can he stand to put that on his head?"

"Paige! Does it have a logo or anything printed on it?"

"Yes. It used to be a gray cap, but now it's just filthy. Printed on the front it says SEWANESCOTT OYSTERS. It's pretty much worn off, though."

"That's great. Now the man himself. Remember: he's not here. He's just in your memory. How tall was he? Was he as tall as I am?" asked Tim.

"Yes," she replied. "Remember, I deal with bodies. I'm good at this. He was around six-feet tall. Thick black hair and a scraggly black beard. He was deeply tanned, like he worked outside, and his eyes were the color of ... well, of oysters. Watery gray. And his hands!"

"What about his hands?"

"They were huge. I've seen hands like that before ... on men that have to pull nets for a living. They get hands that are huge and hard. He had hands like that."

"That's great, Paige. Have you ever seen the man before?"

"I ... I don't ... he looks kind of familiar but ... no, I don't think ... I don't know."

"Have you seen him here, in Eastville?"

"No, I don't think so."

"How about up at your church?"

"No, definitely not."

"In Cape Charles?"

Paige hesitated. Tim held his breath. Maybe they were about to have a breakthrough.

"In Cape Charles?" he asked again.

"Maybe. I may have seen him—"

"Think, Paige."

"Oh, Tim! I think he was one of the men taking the deadrise taxi in from the bunker boat!"

Tim sat back in his chair. Success! Well, at least a lead.

"Okay, Paige. That's great. Now I'm going to wake you up. You'll remember everything we did, and you'll feel very good and very relaxed. Ready? On the count of five. One. Two. Three. Four. Five. You're wide awake."

Paige's eyes opened. She turned to Tim with a huge smile and jumped into his arms.

"Tim! I remembered. I remembered that awful man who kidnapped me. What do we do now? Let's go get him. I want you to hold him while I hang blue crabs on his privates by their claws."

Tim laughed. "Whoa! I don't want to get you mad at *me*. No, we can't just go and pick him up. We don't yet have any actionable proof."

"What about what I just remembered?"

"Not admissible in court. I know you want revenge, but remember I'm an FBI agent. I have to think in terms of laws and bringing him to justice. Besides, you said that he said something about 'the company and the boss.' We want to get the big guys, too. For that, we've got to go carefully and have a plan."

Paige wasn't mollified. "Can I have him first for just a little while? I want to shove stingray spines up under his fingernails."

"Ooo! Geez, girl. Just cool it. He'll get his, but I don't think it will be through your vigilante justice. Let's figure out what we're going to do next, and why they targeted you. That's the main question."

Chapter Twenty-Two

THAT QUESTION WAS bugging Nott, too. Tim had Jim Baugh run by Nott's shack to give him an update, and he was weak with relief. Paige was just a young girl, well woman actually, running a funeral home and acting as a part-time coroner. To the best of Nott's knowledge she wasn't involved in anything evil, unless you considered spending over a dollar for one of those fancy coffees was particularly nefarious. Oh, she had some roughshod ways if you got sideways with her, but not enough to get herself kidnapped and almost killed.

Nott went back to the people he had interviewed about the unidentified skeleton found on the concrete ship. This time he'd watch them real closely and see if he could read anything in them when he told them about what happened to Paige. Maybe one of them did have something to do with it.

He started with Ralph Haynie, the crabber.

Emma Jackson

NOTT FOUND RALPH working his shedding floats. There wasn't much of a breeze and the mosquitoes were having a feast. Nott kept brushing them away from his ears in annoyance.

"You enjoyed sorting peelers so much you came back to help do it some more?"

"No, Mr. Haynie. I wanted to talk to you about my friend, Paige Reese."

"Big Bill's daughter? He and I were Masonic brothers at the Willow Grove Temple down the highway before he passed. I was in his Masonic funeral. How's little Paige doin'?"

Nott replied, "Well, that's what I'd like to talk with you about. Somebody attacked her."

"Attacked her? What happened?"

"Well," said Nott, "someone kidnapped her from her apartment on Wilkins Beach and left her tied up on one of the ships at the Kiptopeke breakwater."

Haynie dropped the net he'd been using. "They what?" he exclaimed. "She okay?"

"She is now, but whoever did it didn't plan on her living to tell the tale. She was left out there for days, tied spread-eagled in the weather."

Haynie shifted his cap and rubbed a forearm over his eyes. "Omigod! Any idea who did it?"

"No," replied Nott. "That's why I'm talking to you. I don't know anyone who'd have it in for Paige. The only thing Paige has been doing lately that's a little different is looking for the name of the person whose skeleton was found out on the concrete ship."

Haynie gave up his work and sat down heavily on a box in his boat. "My gosh! Is that the same ship where they found her?"

"Yeah. Luckily Gordon Campbell was flying a search and Donna Bozza noticed her tied in the exact same place that the skeleton was found. And she was in rough shape, I want to tell you. She'd been there for days with no food or water, sun and rain beating down on her. They flew over and found her, and the Coast Guard sent a helicopter to bring her to the hospital up to Onancock."

Haynie shook his head in wonder.

"Mr. Haynie, you got any idea who might have wanted to hurt Paige like that?"

"Lord no," he replied. "I remember her as a sweet girl. Who'd want to do that? He twisted his weathered fingers together.

"I'll tell you what, though—I'll put the word out at church and through the Masonic brothers, see if anyone has any ideas. How's that?"

"That would be wonderful," said Nott.

"She okay, now?" asked Haynie.

"Well, they let her out of the hospital after a while. She was dehydrated and suffering from some hypothermia. They just left her out there in the rain with no protection. So, she's home taking it easy for now."

Haynie nodded his head, making approving grunts. "Well, you tell her that all us Lodge members'll be praying for her. She need any of the wives to bring anything by?"

"No," said Nott. "She's good. And the women from her church are dropping by with all sorts of food, so she'll be fine. But thanks a lot for caring, Mr. Haynie."

"She need any soft crabs?"

Nott chuckled softly. "Naw," he said. "She's good." And he took his leave while Haynie muttered and fussed over his crab floats.

HE NEXT STOPPED by to talk with Tom Weisiger at his clam farm. He found him elbow-deep in the green algae soup he fed the clams.

"Mr. Weisiger—" Nott started.

"I tol' you to call me 'Tom,' boy."

"Yessir. Sorry. Tom, I don't know if you heard but someone broke into Paige Reese's apartment down on Wilkins Beach and kidnapped her."

"Omigosh! Is she okay?"

"Yessir, she is now. They left her trussed up on one of the ships in the Kiptopeke Breakwater — out in the sun and rain

— for several days. We got Gordon Campbell to fly a search pattern with that little plane he uses for his aerial photography and Donna Bozza spotted her."

"Well, how is she?"

"They called in a Coast Guard 'copter and flew her up to Onancock to Shore Memorial. She was hypothermic and dehydrated but they got her straightened out. She's home now."

Weisiger shook his head. "The stuff that's happening nowadays. Any idea who done it?"

"No sir. That's why I stopped by to talk to you. Have you got any ideas who might want to do such a thing?"

"No," Weisiger said. "I knew her daddy real well through the Masons. Met her at some of the Lodge picnics. Seemed a right sweet little girl. Who'd want to do that to her?"

"Huh! So you're a Mason too?" asked Nott.

"Sure. Can't hardly find any man working on The Shore who isn't in one of the lodges. Me, I was in number 107 along with Big Bill. He was Worshipful Master for a while there. I was working through the chairs."

"The what?"

"Oh! You're not craft, huh? It's just a Masonic thing."

"Uh, huh."

Weisiger smiled. "I'd tell you, but then I'd have to kill you." He chuckled. "You know — us Masons have our secrets."

"I never knew much about the Masons. I mean, I've seen that 'Willow Grove Temple' building out on the highway. But I never talked with anyone about them."

"No, we don't talk much about it to anyone who doesn't belong. It ain't that exclusive, but it is kinda secretive." Weisiger raised his eyebrows and theatrically winked at Nott.

"You know, now I think about it, there was one jasper got blackballed when he tried to join the Lodge. He always blamed Bill Reese, though that kind of thing is a secret."

"Blackballed?"

"Yeah, when someone is applying to join the members have a vote. It only takes one person voting against him to keep him out. That's called a 'blackball'."

"And this guy wanted to join but Bill Reese blackballed him?"

Weisiger furtively looked around as if to check for eavesdroppers. "Well, you see the vote is secret so no one knows who voted how. But this jasper ... what was his name? ... someone dropped the blackball on him and he blamed Big Bill. Got really hot about it. Even threatened to sue the Lodge. 'Course when he found out that most of the judges and attorneys were Masons he just gave up. Damn, what was his name?"

"So you think he might have done this to Paige in revenge for being kept from joining the Masons?" asked Nott.

"Damn if I can think of anyone else, 'cept that deputy who was dating her. And he's dead."

"Yeah," said Nott, remembering the case of the little unknown girl he had found dead in Cherrystone Creek not long ago.

"Wish I could remember that other jasper's name. I'll ask some of the other brothers and see if they remember."

"You think someone could get that mad over not being allowed to join a club?" asked Nott.

"You gotta understand," replied Weisiger. "Masons ain't just a club. I can't go into a lot of detail, but it's a way of life. And if you get blackballed, well, that can affect other things in your life. It's real important to a lot of people."

"Well, that's given me another area to investigate," said Nott. "Thanks, I think. Not sure how I can follow up on this one, not belonging to the Lodge."

"Don't you worry about it, son," replied Weisiger. "Worshipful Master Reese was well-loved. I'll put the word out to the brothers and if there's any connection, we'll find it and tell you. Okay?"

As he drove away from the clam farm Nott was more confused than ever. Not only had he failed to find a suspect for Paige's kidnapping, but he'd also added a new level with this Masonic-thing. He needed to talk to Special Agent Hannegan.

Chapter Twenty-three

THEY MET AT Paige's apartment. Tim and Nott each sipped on a Puddle Pirate Porter as they sat out on the balcony overlooking The Bay. Paige sipped at a highball glass of Cape Charles Maple Whiskey over ice. Despite the still-baffling case, Tim was feeling kind of relaxed. He turned away from looking over the water.

"Nott," Tim started, "we think Paige remembers the man who took her."

"What? Who?" Nott demanded. He looked like he was ready to bring justice on the miscreant himself right now.

Tim half-smiled. "We don't know his name. And we don't really know why he did it, but Paige is pretty sure she remembers him from the wharf in Cape Charles."

Nott was a bit overwhelmed by the big FBI-man, and started out slowly. "Uh, Mr. Hannegan," he stuttered.

Tim quickly interrupted him. "If we're going to get anywhere, Nott, you've got to call me 'Tim.' Understand?"

"Yessir, Special Agent Tim."

Tim sighed. *It's a process*, he thought.

Paige stood. "Gotta go see a man about a seahorse," she said, going back inside.

"What'd you want to talk to me about, Nott?"

"Well, sir ... Tim ... what do you know about ... uh ... secret societies?"

"Secret societies? You mean like gangs? You think maybe MS-13 is trying to get even with Paige for that human trafficking-thing she helped break up?"

"No, no," stuttered Nott. "Like secret clubs and lodges and stuff."

"You mean Freemasons?" asked Tim.

"Yeah. Like them," responded Nott.

"Maybe you'd better tell me from the beginning."

"Well sir ... uh, Tim ... I was asking around, you know, about who might want to hurt Miss Paige? The only common thing I could find was that her daddy, Big Bill Reese? Her daddy once ... uh, kept someone from joining the Masons and the guy got really angry. I've heard that those people, the Masons, have all kinds of secret blood rituals, and I thought maybe that guy was trying to hurt Miss Paige to get even."

"Blood rituals?" asked Tim.

"Yeah, yeah, when I was a kid we were once picking in a field next to that Willow Grove Temple down past Cheriton, and when I asked my daddy about it he warned me to stay away, that it was evil. They practice black magic and worship the devil! Daddy said that they took black and Mexican babies to kill and use their blood and hearts for bad stuff."

Tim smiled at him calmly. "What would you say if I told you that I'm a Mason?"

Nott did a double-take. "Wha'?"

"I've been a member for years, and I've attended lots of different lodges. Sure we've got some secrets but there's honestly nothing going on that deals with blood or babies. Or magic, for that matter."

"But I heard—"

"I know. I've heard it all, too. But I've seen it from the inside, and there's none of that going on. Now, would someone want to get even for being blackballed and not allowed to join? Well, that's a possibility. Who knows what will drive someone into aberrant behavior?"

"Abber — ?"

"Yeah, doing something crazy. Heck, honking at someone at the traffic light might set them off and they shoot you. Doesn't have anything to do with anything. They're just … nuts, and a little thing like that sets them off."

Nott blinked thoughtfully. "Okay. I understand what you're saying. The Masons themselves aren't to blame, but it could be that someone who wanted in and wasn't let in might take that as a reason to act out."

"Right," said Tim. "Unfortunately that just adds another layer of uncertainty and investigation to our work. As if it weren't already so confusing."

Tim turned and called through the open slider into the apartment. "Paige! Can you come out here, please?"

Nott added, "And bring another couple of beers." He smiled at Tim who nodded back.

Paige walked out onto the balcony carrying two more Puddle Pirate Porters for the men and a glass of Church Creek Steel Chardonnay for herself. Putting the drinks down on a glass-topped table she settled herself into the comfortable cushions on an old rattan armchair. Taking a sip of her wine she asked, "So what have you decided?"

Tim said, "Do you remember anything of your daddy's doings with the Masons?"

"The Masons?" she exclaimed. "No, I know that he went down to Willow Grove a couple of times a month and we had family picnics for the members sometimes. Why?"

"Well, one thought we've had is that Big Bill might have blackballed someone who wanted to join, and they're just now trying to get revenge, for some twisted reason," said Tim. "That mean anything to you?"

"Shoot, no," she replied. "Seems like most of Daddy's good friends … heck, most everyone he knew … were members of the lodge. I don't recall any problems. Who told you that?"

"Oh, no one, really," said Nott. He was still worried about the whole secrecy-thing with the Masons.

"No," said Tim, "but when you've got a weird situation like we have here, with no rhyme or reason, then you've gotta start looking at the unlikely scenarios. Sometimes the things that 'just couldn't be it,' turn out to be the answer."

Paige replied, "I get where you're coming from, but I really don't think that you're on the right track. I just don't see how something daddy might have done years ago would result in some nuts kidnapping me today."

"No," said Tim, "probably not. And like you said, 'some nuts.' We're looking for more than one person. If it had been the Masonic-thing, it'd almost certainly be just one perp. You said there were at least two people involved."

"Yeah, it took at least two of them to haul me out to the breakwater and truss me up."

"Guess it must be something else, then," said Nott. "But what? Or who?"

As they sat there on the balcony one of the big menhaden factory boats worked its way by.

"Have you got any binoculars?" asked Tim. "I'd like to watch these guys work."

"I've got a couple of pairs. Let me get them."

Nott and Tim each took a pair of binoculars and focused them on the tableau being acted out in front of them.

Overhead a small spotter airplane, a Cessna 152, circled at around 500 feet. The pilot had seen a moving shadow in the water. A line of brown pelicans, cruising gracefully by on their seven-foot wings, were crashing like bowling balls into the shadow, then emerging with a pouch full of water and fish. It was quite a show. Sometimes the pelicans would crash straight down from seventy feet, their ten-pound bulk pulling them completely under water until they finally emerged, pouch full and a satisfied look on their faces.

The 185-foot mother boat stationed to the bayside of the shadow to hem them in and launched two 40-foot purse boats. Between them these two boats had a net, 1800-feet long, with which they surrounded the shadowy school of fish. This was the purse seine, a curtain of net that would be hauled in by the mother boat, tightening a line that closed the bottom of the net like a purse preventing any fish from escaping.

Tim and Nott watched this boat-ballet with interest. Nott was amused that during this case he had learned about crabbing and clam farming and pound fishing, and now he was learning about purse seining. He was becoming a regular white-boot waterman.

As they watched, the net was pulled up and aboard the mother boat, concentrating the fish into one living squirming mass. Then a huge pump was used to suck the fish out of the net and into the belly of the factory ship where they struggled in a dense pack.

Once the net had been emptied the purse boats were winched back aboard, in this case up ramps located at the stern of the factory ship, and off they went looking for another school of fish.

"That's a slick operation," observed Tim. "And what all are they fishing for?"

Paige replied ruefully, "Well, they are fishing for menhaden. Bunkers. That's it. They're an oily trash fish not good for eating, and they take them to a factory over across The Bay where they extract the oil and grind up the bodies for fertilizer and animal feed."

"If they're no good for eating, and you called them a 'trash fish,' then it's good they found a use for them, right?"

"Hmmph," grumped Paige. It'd be good if that was all they caught, I suppose. But that big net of theirs sweeps up anything that's in the water. Bunkers, cobia, trout, flounder ... anything swimming. They're not supposed to. It's against regulations, actually. But by the time they finally sort through the catch and extract the non-bunkers, they've been bashed around so much they're usually dead. Then when they throw them back in, they just float up dead on the beach."

"That's what Mr. Weisiger and Jason Duke were talking about. They called it 'bycatch'," said Nott.

"That's what it is," said Paige. And if they are fishing too close to the beach the bycatch becomes a garbage problem.

"Or sometimes they'll catch a net on something and tear it."

"Mr. Duke talked about that, too. He told me that he's been scuba diving in The Bay for years and he's seen where the nets have gotten hung up on the coral and both shredded the net and torn up the coral. He's really steamed about it."

Paige nodded her head. "A lot of us are. We try to get the regulators to do something, but money talks and the menhaden industry has lots of high-priced lobbyists in Richmond. You know, Virginia is the only state that allows menhaden fishing inside The Bay. All other states insist that it be done in the open ocean. But we just keep pissing away a valuable resource."

Tim was shocked. He wasn't used to hearing Paige talk so vehemently about any subject. He resolved to look more deeply into the menhaden industry when he had the time.

Chapter Twenty-Four

A FEW DAYS later Tim called with news about the skeleton. Since that case seemed to intersect with Paige's kidnapping, he fudged jurisdiction a bit and insisted that DNA from the skeleton and the hair sample be sent to the FBI forensic lab in Quantico, Virginia. They administered the massive database of the National DNA Index System (NDIS). If the victim had ever been in the military, or if he had a federal arrest or a civil arrest in many states, his DNA would be on file. They had finally called back with a hit from their database.

"So who was it?" asked Paige.

"According to our lab, the bones belong to one Jon Dickson."

"The bones?" Paige asked. "The hair, too?"

"No," answered Tim. "Not the hair."

It turned out that the skeleton belonged to one Jon Dickson. He'd been in the military data base of the NDIS, having served as a photojournalist in the Coast Guard for eight years. But what did that tell them? Tim wasn't sure. He decided to brainstorm it with Paige and Nott over on The Shore.

"Jon Dickson?" asked Paige. "I've never heard of him."

"He's apparently from this side of The Bay," said Tim. "I've got an address for him, but it's in a pretty run-down part of Portsmouth. He was renting a studio in a house that's old enough to be in the historic district, but instead is just rundown.

"Studio? He was an artist?"

"No, he fancied himself an investigative reporter," said Tim. "I've got a search warrant and I'm going over there now to check it out."

"Let me know if you find anything," said Paige. "But what about the hair sample? Any DNA hits on that?"

"No, the hair was definitely not Dickson," replied Tim, "but we didn't get any hits on who it was. Nothing in the data bases."

TIM AND A team of forensic experts from the Norfolk FBI office drove to the Portsmouth address for Jon Dickson. It was a huge old house that probably would have been included in the historic district if it hadn't been divided up into apartments many years ago. There was a large porch on the front overlooking the street with a chain-suspended porch swing and several old and weathered rocking chairs. None of the furniture had seen a paintbrush for a long time. A series of rusty mailboxes flanked the screened front door and bled orange rust down the white-painted clapboard wall. All-in-all it was an unprepossessing place.

The front door was standing open so they went in and found that the live-in manager's apartment was on the left in what had originally been a sitting room and kitchen. A large staircase stretched up before them, the old wooden steps scarred and worn, and several of the balusters missing on the banister.

Tim showed the search warrant to the manager, and he led them to a tiny attic studio on the third floor. He said that he hadn't seen the resident for a few months, but since he was an investigative journalist he figured he was gone working on a story. His rent was paid automatically from a bank account so the super hadn't thought much about his absence. Indeed, unless there was something broken he stayed in his own apartment and paid no attention to his tenants. Tim could smell the alcohol on his breath. The manager unlocked and opened the door then stepped back. Tim thanked him, then pointedly stared at him until he felt uncomfortable enough to take the hint and leave. He returned downstairs to his own quarters.

Just as he had done at Paige's apartment Tim didn't let his forensic crew in, but started the search by simply standing in the open doorway and letting the apartment "speak" to him. Paige's apartment hadn't had much to say. This place did.

The studio apartment consisted of just one room and looked to have been decorated by a tornado. But as Tim examined it from the doorway it become obvious that the room had been tossed by someone searching for something. There was a distinct difference between the mess left by a sloppy bachelor and a methodic searching and trashing. Drawers were emptied on the floor, clothes had been pulled from the closet, the bed *cum* couch had been overturned, and the little work area with its door-on-sawhorses desk was destroyed. Tim noted that there were no journals or notebooks lying in the office clutter, and though there was a printer and a power strip there was no computer or laptop. *That's strange,* Tim mused. *A reporter with no writing machine nor research notes? Was he really a reporter?*

There were board-and-brick bookshelves, but they had been dumped and all of the books lay scattered on the floor. "You see that?" Tim asked his team. "Those books haven't just been pulled out, they've been riffled through to make certain there's nothing secreted in the pages."

The cabinets and drawers in the tiny kitchen were open, their contents dumped on the floor. "How on earth did all this damage take place with no one hearing it?" asked one of the techs.

"There's no one else living up here in the attic," answered Tim. "Plus it's an old house. It might be beat up now, but the floors are still thick. Unless they stomped around, the people living downstairs probably wouldn't have heard anything. But just in case, one of you guys go down and interview whoever lives directly below here." A male tech left.

With no computer nor work product to look at, it was difficult to guess what Dickson had been researching. There seemed to be no clues. Even the fingerprint tech was frustrated—everything seemed to have been wiped down with not even Dickson's prints in evidence.

Then Tim saw a corner of paper sticking out from between the desktop and one of the supporting sawhorses. Donning a pair of black Nitrile gloves and using tweezers he gently removed what turned out to be a business card. *Wayne Creed, Editor. Cape Charles Mirror, Cape Charles, Virginia.*

"Find something?" asked the fingerprint tech.

"Something, but I'm not sure what," answered Tim. "But at least it's a lead. You guys finish up here and let me know if you find anything interesting. I'm heading back across to Cape Charles and see if I can track down this Wayne Creed fellow."

On his way back across the Bridge-Tunnel, Tim called Paige. "Do you know a 'Wayne Creed'?"

"Sure I do. He lives down in Cape Charles and publishes an online newspaper, *The Cape Charles Mirror*. Why?"

"I found one of his business cards in Dickson's apartment. Actually, it was about the only thing I *did* find worth mentioning. The place looked like Hurricane Darrell had gone through it. Twice. There were no papers or journals about what he was doing, and his computer was gone."

"Wow," said Paige. "Well, Wayne's a real nice guy. I'm sure he'll be happy to talk with you."

Wayne Creed met with Tim at his home. He was a pleasant-looking middle-aged man, graying at the temples, and with a hint of a dimple in the point of his chin. He was dressed in khakis and a blue sweatshirt. The interview was congenial but somewhat unfruitful. Yes, he knew Jon Dickson. No, he didn't work for him, but Wayne had offered to look at any of his investigative stuff and see whether he wanted to publish it or not.

"He's a nice boy," said Wayne. "A veteran. He had a burr under his saddle about environmental things, though. But, heck, you live over here on The Shore and on the water, you pretty much have to be an environmentalist. We live close to the land, and we value it. So I told him that if he wanted to consider himself a stringer for *The Mirror*, it was good by me. Gave him one of my business cards to give him a little cachet, maybe help him get into some places he might not be able to otherwise."

"Do you know what he'd been working on recently?" asked Tim.

"Well, I haven't seen the boy in quite some time. What's this all about?"

"Mr. Creed, you can't report this yet, but it looks as though the skeleton that was found on the Kiptopeke Breakwater was Jon Dickson."

"NO!"

"We identified his DNA through the military database."

"Well ... I never! Now, who'd want to do that? Was it an accident?"

"We sincerely don't think so. He had apparently been tied spread-eagle to some fittings on the ship."

"Oh, my!"

"So, I'll ask you again," Tim continued, "any ideas about what he was investigating?"

Wayne thought for a while. "He had a couple of things in the hopper that I know of. He was interested in the possibility of someone coming in and putting up a wind farm in the Atlantic around the barrier islands. They're owned by the Nature Conservancy, so the windmills would have had to be offshore. He was concerned with what that might do to migratory birds. You know, we are a major flyway for Canada geese, as well as our pelicans and terns and laughing gulls. We've finally got a few bald eagles back to nesting in the wildlife refuge. You know, the Fish and Wildlife people say that there are 406 species of birds that use our refuge, so we're real interested in protecting them." Creed sounded like a representative of the Chamber of Commerce Visitor's Bureau.

"Okay. That's interesting, but is there anything actually happening, yet, as far as the wind farm?"

"Well, no, not really. Some people were really hot about it a while ago, but that seems to have petered out some. Not enough return on investment, I heard."

"What else?" Tim asked.

Wayne thought. "Well, there are those people that rebuilt the marina, Mallard Cove?"

"He's got something against them?"

"Well, no. Not really. I think he'd be happier if they weren't there at all, but I guess I never did hear him say anything. And they're just fixing up an old place that's been there for years. I suppose that's nothing. And they seem to be real conscious of the environment around them, protecting it and all."

"Okay, Mr. Creed. Please, think hard. What else might Jon Dickson have been investigating?"

"Maybe Bay Creek," he offered quietly.

"Bay Creek?" asked Tim.

"Yeah, it's a big development with golf courses and lots of homes. Just south of Cape Charles."

"And Dickson was investigating them?"

"We-e-e-ll, no, not really. They were going great guns when they first started. Even got Nicklaus and Palmer to design their two golf courses. You play golf? You know, we used to have a little course right here in town. Northampton Country Club. It was just a little thing with nine holes, but it was kind of convenient and cheap. Course it went away with all the new construction. Lots of people bought big homes in Bay Creek. A lot of them on speculation, but then the market for big vacation homes kind of went soft, and with the bridge tolls to come over from the western shore being so high … I think a lot of people lost money."

"Mr. Creed," said Tim. "Please focus here. Was Jon Dickson investigating something at Bay Creek?"

"Well, no, I don't think so. I'm just trying to think of other things down here that might have interested him."

Tim turned away. "Okay, Mr. Creed. I appreciate your time. If you think of anything else, you be sure to call me. I left you my card." He started to walk off.

"Wait a minute," said Creed. "Pogies!"

"Pogies?"

"Yeah, pogies. Mossbunkers. MENHADEN! Jon had a real sore spot for the bunker industry. I told him that he could act as a stringer for us if he uncovered something about the menhaden fishing industry, either good or bad. That's got to be it!"

Chapter Twenty-Five

POGIES! WHO DID they know who could fill them in on the menhaden fishing industry? Tim talked it over with Paige and they decided to detail Nott to look into it. After all, he was a male, and if he returned to his previous clothing he could easily pass for a down-at-the-mouth commercial fisherman.

"Gee, I don't know," said Nott when they talked with him about their plan. "I don't know nothing about commercial fishin', and I sure don't know no one that works on one of them big boats."

"We'll start you with doing research online," said Tim. "That way you can get some background before you have to do any one-on-one. Okay?"

"I ain't got a computer," said Nott. "Don't rightly know how to use one, neither."

"I've got a laptop you can use either in the upstairs apartment at the funeral home or at my apartment on the beach," said Paige. "And teaching you to use Google and other search engines will be easy."

"Search *engines?*" asked Nott. "What're those?"

Tim and Paige got Nott set up on the kitchen table of the apartment in Eastville. The internet down at the beach was still too iffy, and they didn't want to take the risk of wasting time. Paige showed him how to log in, and how to search for articles about menhaden fishing. She and Tim put their heads together and also came up with a list of keywords that Nott could use for his searches: menhaden, mossbunkers, bunkers, pogies, Chesapeake Bay, commercial fishing, purse-seining and the like. They told him to find articles he thought were pertinent, read them, and if they really looked important print them out on the little ink jet printer that was hooked to the computer. They also taught him how he could use keywords found in the articles to spread and deepen his search.

"Sounds kinda cool," said Nott. "Learning a new skill."

"Then when you've learned enough to sound knowledgeable we'll have you talk to Wayne Creed at the CAPE CHARLES MIRROR and see what else he can add. And maybe go back and talk with Jason Duke out to Smith Beach," said Paige, while Nott nodded his head and started punching keys with his index fingers on the laptop computer.

"And while you're doing that, I've got to go back to my office and do some paperwork," said Tim. "This still isn't officially in my jurisdiction, so I need to keep the 'boys upstairs' happy with where I'm spending my time." He looked at Paige.

"There's been some muttering that I'm spending so much time over here because of you."

Paige blushed prettily. "I can't imagine what they mean."

Tim laughed. "Okay, then. Nott, you've got your marching orders, and Paige ... what are you going to do?"

Paige snorted a laugh. "If you remember, I do have a funeral business to run. I don't make any money out of this Agatha Christie stuff. I'll have plenty to do until we come up with some more leads to follow."

Tim leaned forward and planted a kiss on the tip of her nose, then went down the stairs to his car. As she listened to the crunch of gravel under his departing tires Paige gave a little sigh and went downstairs to her office.

NOTT SPENT HOURS searching the Internet and reading everything he could find about menhaden and the industry that fished for and used them. He hadn't read this much since he had been in classes in the Army, and he was developing a massive headache when Paige came back upstairs with two Cobb Island IPAs.

"Beer!" exclaimed Nott as he popped the top off one of the bottles. "You don't know how much I need this."

"Are you learning a lot about bunker fishing?" asked Paige.

"More than you can imagine," he replied. "But an awful lot of the stuff is published by the industry itself. Makes them sound just as pure as the driven snow."

"Hmmph. That may be," she answered. "But that's why we've gotta talk to other people, too."

"I know what you mean," said Nott. "I know when I was talking to Jack Long, the pound fisherman, he said that used to be he caught lots of bunkers in his pound nets and sold them for bait. Not no more. He seemed pretty put out about it."

"See? That's what I mean. Sure, the PR guys in the industry aren't goin' to say anything bad. We gotta talk to other people who're not in the industry but are affected by it."

"Like Jason Duke?"

"Like Jason Duke."

That night, after dark, Paige called Jason Duke at his home.

"Mr. Duke, this is Paige Reese up to Eastville."

"Yeah?"

"Mr. Duke, I don't know if you're aware but I'm the acting county coroner," she paused.

"Yeah?" He was responsive but certainly not affable.

"And I'm working on a murder right now where I think you might be able to help me."

"Murder! I don't know nobody been murdered. Whatta you mean?"

"Well sir, I'm not sure but I think it might be connected to the menhaden fishing industry, and I need to talk with someone who can give me an unbiased opinion."

Duke's raucous laughter over the phone was almost ear-splitting. "Unbiased?" he yelled. "And you're coming to me? Girl, I'm about as biased as they come. I hate those people. Yeah, I'll talk to you."

"Mr. Duke, what I'd like to do is send my friend, Nott Smith, out tomorrow morning to talk with you. You've met him before."

"Yeah, sure. I know the boy. Tell him to be here around seven tomorrow morning. And tell him to bring some sticky buns from Kates Kupboard up to Exmore when he comes. If I'm gonna be interviewed, that's how I'll be paid for it."

"Yessir," said Paige. "Will do."

THE FUNERAL HOME'S pickup truck with Nott at the wheel pulled into Duke's yard at Smith Beach early the next morning and parked next to Duke's big king-cab pickup. Nott was almost drowning in drool because of the smell of the freshly-baked cinnamon buns still hot in their box on the passenger seat. Grabbing the box, he hurried to the front door, which opened before he even got there.

"Coffee?" asked Jason Duke.

"Uh, yes, please," responded Nott.

"Damn those things smell good," said Duke. "Ever since that girl agreed to have you bring 'em I've been hankering for them."

"Yessir."

"Bring your coffee and we'll go sit on the deck out back. I've been tracking one of the bunker boats this morning and he's right off the beach. I'll tell you all 'bout them and show you, too."

Holding his scalding hot mug of coffee Nott followed Duke out the back door and out to the deck that sat some fifteen feet above the beach at the top of an eroded bank. They sat in canvas captain's chairs and Duke handed a pair of binoculars to Nott. "There they are," he said, pointing south.

Nott didn't need the binoculars to see that the large factory boat was less than a mile south of them and close-in to shore.

"Uh, aren't they too close to the beach?" he asked.

Duke spit over the edge of the bank, then took a big bite of cinnamon bun. "Over on the other side, they's what they call a 'gentleman's agreement' that they stay at least three miles off the Virginia Beach Oceanfront. That's where all the money is. And they stay away from Lynnhaven Inlet 'cause that's where the rich charter boats are. But over here they's just us farmers with no political clout, so they snuggle right on up."

"Does that hurt anything?" asked Nott.

Duke looked at him with a combination of dismay and disgust.

"Let me explain the whole process to you." He slurped a mouthful of coffee and swallowed, sighing with satisfaction.

"You see that little plane circling up there?"

"Yeah."

"That little Cessna 172 is a spotter plane for this factory boat. He flies at about 500 feet. Bunkers swim in a dense school, usually kind of shallow, so the spotter plane looks for 'shadows' in the water. They also look for gulls and pelicans diving on the school. Once they see a school of fish they estimate how many fish are in the school, maybe around 60,000 fish, and they radio the mother boat. They'll race over to the school and launch two 40' purse boats. Each purse boat has one-half of an 1800-foot long purse net in it. They'll go opposite directions and spread that net around the school of fish.

"Once the school is encircled the mother ship will haul on a line that closes the bottom of the net just like an old-timey change purse, and the fish are stuck. They'll winch in the net, concentrating the school of fish into a dense mass, then they'll use a vacuum to actually suck them out of the net and into the ship's hold."

"That's pretty slick," said Nott. "And all of the fish in the school are just menhaden?"

"No," said Duke, "and that's one of the problems I have with them. That net sweeps up anything that's there. The bunkers, of course, but any bluefish or spot or trout or croaker or stripers or any other fish unlucky enough to be in the neighborhood. They call that 'bycatch'."

"Don't they throw that back?"

"They're supposed to. But by the time they separate out the bycatch from the 9 tons of menhaden, mostly it's dead. They throw it overboard, 'cause they don't want it, but it's just wasted." Duke shook his head and spit toward the offending ship.

"Oh! Take the binoculars and look down there now. See that rush of water being shot out the side?"

Nott nodded.

"When they use the vacuum to empty the fish out of the net it sucks up a lot of water, too. The fish themselves settle to the bottom of the holds and that excess water is pumped out and overboard to make room for more fish. That's called the 'bail water,' and as well as just water it contains fish waste and scales and stuff and is considered a pollutant. It forms a slime line and if they are too close to the beach that slime line washes up onto the sand."

"Yuck."

"No kidding. I have grandkids who come to visit and like to play on the beach. But if those bunker boats have been around ... I sometimes can't allow it."

"Okay, so you have dead fish from the bycatch and the slime line. That's all pretty bad. Anything else?"

"Oh, Lordy! Lots." He paused to take another bite of cinnamon roll and wash it down with another slug of coffee.

"As a kid I used to dive in the same area where that boat is to watch bottom feeders and coral formations. They're all gone now along with the small crabs and fish which used to live in the habitat. The menhaden commercial boats have destroyed the bottom with their equipment and their waste water washing up on our beaches. Just last year there were three gigantic fish spills from their nets with the dead fish on our beaches. I also have written and spoken to Virginia State officials and they have done nothing. Our Chesapeake Bay is a fragile environment. Get the menhaden commercial boats out of The Bay! Maryland and Delaware and New Jersey don't let them fish their bays." He glowered fiercely at the boat for a long moment.

"Actually, boy, just last year one of the boat's nets caught on something close to the sand bar and it tore open spilling thousands of fish, now dead, which washed up on the beaches. A commercial clean-up crew walked the beaches and picked up the dead fish which had washed in. That cleans up the beach, but doesn't do crap for the sport fishing. They fish so close to the shore their nets drag on the bay bottom tearing up the natural corals, sea grasses, and bottom habitat."

"My gosh," said Nott. "And no one stops them?"

"They've got the lobbying money. No one wants to upset the apple cart. I'm one of the few who keep after them." Duke licked his fingers enjoying the sticky cinnamon.

"I don't want to sound like a nut case, but—"

"No," said Nott. "I read online about how the menhaden are important food for other fish, too, and that some fish scientists say that stocks of stripers and other gamefish have decreased as menhaden fishing increased. Is that true?"

"I ain't a scientist and I don't know for sure, but I sure know that the fishing in The Bay ain't nothing like it was when I was a kid. The Chesapeake is fragile, and we're killing it."

By now the dregs of the coffee were cold and the sticky buns were all gone. Nothing left but sticky fingers to lick. Nott stuck out his hand. "Captain, I appreciate your time and the education."

"Boy, I don't know if what you're doin' will do anything to control those pirates, but I sure wish you luck."

"Thank you, sir," said Nott, and he drove back into town to the apartment above the funeral home. He'd found a possible corporate villain, but how to decide specifically who and what and when? And especially, why.

Chapter Twenty-Six

"DO YOU REALLY think they would commit murder over fishing?" asked Paige as the three of them sat on the balcony of her apartment. They watched as a scruffy old cat walked across the grass below, trying to ignore the dive-bombing mockingbird that kept pecking him on the head.

Nott had just briefed Paige and Tim about his meeting with Duke and the man's virulent hate for the menhaden industry.

"Yeah," he replied. "Apparently there are up to three generations working together on some of them factory boats. That makes it a family business. I can imagine them being real protective of their heritage. Shoot, my daddy was a nothing farmworker and I ain't got no idea who my granddaddy was. Ain't no history there. But I knew some guys in the Army who kept talking about gettin' home and joining what they called 'the family business.' Seemed real proud of it."

"Hmm," said Tim. "Yeah, I guess I can see that. My father and his father were both cops. I've got a brother who is a police sergeant down in south Florida, and my sister is on the New York State Highway Patrol. Law enforcement is kind of our family business, and we're all proud of it. I can guess how much more important it would be to us if we were all stationed at the same precinct house."

"Makes sense to me," said Paige. "I'm working in the family business ... not that I really wanted to be, but when my daddy died the choices were: come back to run the family business or close it down. I couldn't do that. So ... I guess I can see some hot-headed crewman maybe killing to protect his family work heritage. But, still, why Dickson and especially why me?"

Tim said, "Dickson first. We know that he was an investigative reporter. That means that he looked for the underbelly of things." He stopped and scanned the notes he had taken on a yellow legal pad. "From what I've read on the Internet the menhaden industry is at odds with the State of Virginia. In 2017 the state followed the recommendations of the Atlantic States Marine Fisheries Commission and cut its bay quota of menhaden caught to 51,000 tons annually. No other states even allow purse seining for menhaden in their bays. But the industry said that the cap was too low, and the feds accused them of exceeding the cap by 400 tons *in the bay*. That's 800,000 pounds of fish. That has the environmentalists up in arms, and is just the thing that a young rabble-rouser like Dickson could sensationalize in the press."

"I knew they were unpopular," said Paige, "but I didn't know about those numbers."

"Then there's the bycatch, that Nott told us about, and the bail water and slime line."

"But still, Tim, is that worth murdering Dickson? And why come after me?"

"Paige, if what I'm seeing here adds up to a violation of state regulations and possible financial manipulations of state legislators by lobbyists, as well as violations of federal clean water regulations, we could be looking at what the FBI would consider a criminal enterprise. Since his notes and computer disappeared we don't know what Jon Dickson found in his investigation, but if it was along these lines, then it would be well worth killing to protect."

"But why me?" Paige complained.

"Well, I guess they thought that they were home safe when Dickson's body was never found until it became just an unknown skeleton on the breakwater. If no one knew who he was, or what he was doing, they wouldn't be able to follow the string back to the menhaden industry.

"Figure it like this: Dickson thought he had a juicy story about legislative corruption. He got himself hired on as a worker on a menhaden boat."

"Wait a minute," said Nott. "How do you figure that?"

"The best way to develop solid information is by being inside. Remember: his skeleton was found wearing fisherman's boots. He most likely got himself into the company as a fisherman." Nott nodded his head in understanding.

"But wouldn't that be dangerous?" asked Paige.

"Of course," said Tim. "But a young reporter thinks he is invincible." He shook his head ruefully.

"Then, from his vantage point on board one of the factory boats he watched and took notes. The notes that we couldn't find in his apartment but someone else did. If we look we can probably find where he traveled to Richmond for research into the lobbying doings. Matter-of-fact, once I get this officially recognized as an FBI case, that's what I'll have a team do.

"Somehow the powers-that-be heard about his investigation—heard that he was a reporter—and decided to eliminate the problem. There's almost certainly no trail that we can follow, but I imagine that someone in management mentioned the pesky reporter that they found snooping around, and how he was trying to hurt the company and how that would risk jobs, and it trickled down from there until it got to a level where someone, in order to protect their jobs, took him out."

"My goodness," said Paige. "What do we do now?"

"For starters," said Tim, "I'd like to confront that fisherman who kidnapped you. We can then see where we go from there."

"How are we going to do that?" asked Nott. "We don't have any legal proof of anything. Unless he is dumb enough to agree to talk with us, he can just walk off."

"That's true enough," said Tim. "So we're going to have to be clever. And we might have to step over the line to do so. Are y'all ready to … stretch the law a bit?"

Paige smiled with one eyebrow raised. "Let's do it."

Chapter Twenty-Seven

THAT FRIDAY NIGHT, at around nautical twilight, Nott was standing leaning against a light post on the Cape Charles Harbor dock while Tim and Paige sat in Tim's car about fifty yards away. As soon as he heard the deadrise taxi boat coming in he pushed the speed dial for Tim and slid the phone into his front pocket. They had contacted Jim Baugh and he was standing by in his flats boat over at King's Creek Marina. Tim had brought a small Sabre stun gun from his office, and Nott gripped it tightly his pocket.

Tim had been very specific about the use of the stun gun. "When you have him in your scow," he told Nott, give a little jolt with the stun gun. Not a big jolt. Just enough to disorient him."

Paige piped up. "Can I use that stun gun on his privates?"

Tim laughed. "Maybe later. Actually, I don't want him to see you yet."

He turned to Nott. "Nott, tie his wrists securely, and run him out to your shack. You'll want to tie his hands in front of him so he can use them to climb out of the boat and up to the shack, but be real careful. Keep the stun gun where he can see it. Intimidate him. You could actually touch it to his neck without pushing the button just to remind him."

Nervously Nott nodded his understanding.

Tim continued. "Once you get him up into your shack, start asking him about the skeleton and about Paige. You don't need *professionally interrogate* him. Just ask him enough to get him to deny knowing anything. I want you to have this cell phone in your pocket turned on and connected with mine. That way I'll be able to listen in to what's happening."

Again Nott nodded. Paige was beginning to fidget.

"Okay, it's showtime." Paige and Tim melted back into the shadows.

The deadrise approached the dock and Nott caught the tossed bow line holding it to the dock as the three passengers climbed out. Then he tossed it back aboard as the deadrise reversed and headed out of the harbor.

None of the three men even looked at Nott, much less thanked him. Nott's target was the long rangy one. As they started walking away Nott tugged on the sleeve of his target and said, "Hey, can you come over to my boat? I found this thing on the beach and I don't know what it is. Might be a piece of a missile, or something. Maybe one of those jets headed for the Navy base dropped it, and we could get a reward." He started walking over to his scow and the man slowly followed.

"Where's it at?" he growled.

"I covered it over with that piece of tarp so no one would see it. You know, in case it is worth something. Didn't want nobody takin' it away from me. Really didn't want no law to see it."

They climbed into the scow and the man bent down to lift the tarp. As he did so Nott put the prongs of the stun gun against his neck and pushed the button.

The results were both spectacular and gratifying. There was no lightning nor crackling blue sparks, but a mild click followed by a buzz. Instantly the man straightened as his muscles violently contracted. His mouth opened wide and issued a gargling shout. He then fell forward face-first, his body almost vibrating, into the tarp. Still yelling his face hit the bottom of the boat, though it was cushioned by the tarp.

Grabbing a short piece of line Nott flipped the man onto his back and roughly lashed his wrists together. The man was conscious, but did not yet have control of his muscles. Drool ran down the side of his mouth. As his eyes focused on Nott he rasped, "What the hell—?" Nott waved the stun gun at him and he flinched away. Nott tossed the tarp over him.

Starting his outboard Nott quickly untied his bow and stern lines and, waving to Tim and Paige in the waiting car, then pulled away from the dock heading out into The Bay and up to his Oyster shack on Cherrystone Creek.

The man under the tarp was yelling and struggling, but a swift kick and a snarled warning from Nott calmed him down. Until they got to Nott's shack.

IN THE CAR Tim and Paige kept an eye on Nott until they saw him pull away from the dock. They then rushed over to King's Creek Marina and met up with Jim and his shallow-draft flats boat. Idling out of King's Creek toward The Bay they watched until they saw Nott motor by, then pulled in to follow him in trail. Nott knew they were there but they stayed far enough back so they wouldn't be noticed as Nott got his passenger up into the shack They had told him to have the man sit on the floor of the shack with his back to the door, tied hands in his lap.

Tim and Paige drew close enough to slip onto the steps and peek in through the cracks in the wall. The voices came through clearly.

"**YOU KNOW ANYTHING** 'bout that skeleton found on the breakwater ship?" asked Nott.

The man just looked up him, scowling, and muttered something under his breath.

"Whadja say?" asked Nott.

"I said f**k you," snarled the man.

Nott followed Tim's directions and just smiled broadly and nodded his head. *This piece of trash,* he thought to himself.

"How 'bout Paige Reese? Know her?"

The man smiled grimly. "I don't know who you're talking about, you—"

Again, Nott just smiled and nodded at the man.

"Are you simple?" the man asked. "Say something. Don't just nod and smile like a nincompoop."

Nincompoop, thinks Nott. *I'm not the one tied up sitting on the floor. I'm not the one who killed two people.* He keeps smiling and nodding, and the man on the floor likely keeps wondering what is going on.

"You better untie me and let me outta here. Who the hell do you think you are?"

DEEP SHADOWS COVER the interior of the shack. The only illumination comes from a simple candle lantern hanging from a nail. The furniture is basic, a camp cot and a camp chair that looks like it has been scavenged from the beach. There's a rough table and some shelves hanging on the wall holding cans of food, much of it Dinty Moore Beef Stew.

There's a sudden breeze and he hears the door of the shack quietly close behind him. He tries to wrench around to see who has come in, but only sees a shadowy form. "Who the hell are you?" he snarls.

The shadow moves around into the light of the candle lantern, and the man on the floor starts violently.

"You! You can't be here. You're dead."

"I am?" asked Paige mildly.

"I saw you there. I tied you up on the boat. There weren't no way you could have slipped those knots."

"I couldn't?" asked Paige, smiling quietly.

The man on the floor quickly looked from Paige to Nott and back again to Paige. "What's happening here?" he asked querulously.

Paige's look hardened. "What's your name?" she demanded.

"What?"

"What—is—your—name?"

"Uh, Billy Ray. Billy Ray Simpkins."

"All right, Billy Ray, why'd you try to kill me?"

He started to snivel. "Kill you? I ain't never tried to kill you. What you talkin' 'bout?"

Paige turned to Nott and he handed her the stun gun.

"Whoa, wait a minute," said Billy Ray, and he scooted back away from her on the splintery floor. "I didn't do no harm to you."

"No? How about I leave you naked, tied up on one of those ships? Or how about I just fry your oysters with this little gadget? Nott, take his drawers down."

"NOW WAIT A MINUTE," Billy Ray yelled. "You can't do that to me. That ain't legal."

"Who says I gotta care about 'legal'?" asked Paige. "Tying me up and leaving me on the breakwater wasn't exactly legal, was it?"

Billy Ray now had snot running down his face as he continued sniveling. He turned his head and wiped it on his shoulder. "Now, you're a girl. You can't go doin' things like that."

Paige smiled in grim satisfaction as Billy Ray said the things guaranteed to piss her off enough to sizzle him. She advanced on him with the stun gun.

"Why'd you kill the boy?" She abruptly changed the direction of her questioning.

Billy Ray's mind was too addled by all that was happening and too scared of further shocks from the stun gun. "D-do what?" he stuttered out.

"That reporter boy. Jon Dickson. Why'd you kill him?"

"I-I-I don't know what you're talkin' 'bout."

"Come on, Billy Ray. You bragged to me that you were going to leave me right where we found the Dickson boy's skeleton. How'd you know that if you weren't involved with killing him?"

"I didn't kill nobody," Billy Ray protested. "I mighta tied him up there, but I never killed him."

Nott nodded his head. "Left him to die, but didn't actually kill him, huh? Think that lets you off the hook?"

"No," Paige said, "he was strangled. That's how he died. And you did it."

"He mighta fell when we were putting him out there and hit his throat when he went down. That mighta done it. I didn't choke him."

Paige called out, "Heard enough, Tim?"

The door opened again and in stepped Hannegan.

"Tim Hannegan, FBI, I'd like you to meet Billy Ray Simpkins, waterman, kidnapper, and murderer."

Billy Ray goggled up at the towering special agent. "Uh ..."

"I just happened to be in a fishing boat under the shack when I heard voices. So I listened in, being nosy, and I heard what you were saying, my friend. So, before I talk with you, let me read you your rights."

Tim produced a card from his badge wallet and read it to Billy Ray. "Do you understand these rights as I've read them to you?"

"Now wait just a damned minute," sputtered Billy Ray. "This guy over here attacked me with a weapon of some sort and then kidnapped me. Then this girl threatened to zap me in my privates unless I told her that I'd done stuff I never. This is all wrong. Y'all cain't do this to me. Ain't right."

This time it was Tim who just smiled and nodded at Billy Ray. "I'm sure the judge will take all of your complaints into consideration and weigh them against your assault, kidnapping, and murder charges."

"Can't I please zap him in the *huevos* now?" asked Paige. "Just once to pay him back for what he did to me?"

Tim held out his hand for the stun gun and smiling said, "Paige, I know you'd love a little payback. Let's see how things go with Billy Ray. He might need some encouragement to help out later on."

Billy Ray's head whipped back and forth between Tim and Paige. "You keep her away from me," he cried. "She ain't right!"

Chapter Twenty-Eight

THEY WERE IN a good place. Billy Ray, as dumb as a clam, was way off balance. He honestly wasn't sure who had him, where he was or what they knew. The only thing that he was certain of was that the girl kept threatening to turn him into a soprano, and that scared him.

The big man, the others had called him Tim, just stood staring at him, nodding, a mysterious smile on his face.

"Whadya want with me?" he demanded, though without a lot of conviction in his voice.

"You know what we want," said the tall man. "Who put you up to all this? You're not smart enough to have done it all on your own, are you?"

"No! I ... wait ... are you callin' me ignerant? I ain't dumb."

"So you did commit murder, kidnapping, attempted murder, assault and other crimes on your own?"

"Hey! I never said that," protested a now thoroughly confused Billy Ray.

"If all of this wasn't your idea, then whose was it?"

"I ain't sayin'," stated a recalcitrant Billy Ray.

"Fine by me," said Tim. "Makes my job easier."

"Whadya mean?"

"Oh, I've got you dead to rights. Convince me that there's no one else, and I'll just go with you. Unfortunatly for you, though. The murder of Jon Dickson is a state offense. But Virginia will let you choose whether you want to be electrocuted or die by lethal injection. I hear that the electric chair is faster, but sometimes it takes a couple of jolts. Sometimes it even sets you on fire."

Billy Ray's eyes goggled. He frantically shook his head and looked around the shack for help. There was none there for him.

"Now, if this all went higher than just you being stupid, then it might become a federal crime and if you're just a small cog in this, then you might not be executed. Interesting, huh?"

"You're jest tryin' to get to me," whined Billy Ray.

Tim leaned in close and in his best John Wayne rasp said, "I AM getting to you."

Billy Ray sat there sniveling. "I 'uz jest followin' orders," he said.

"Billy Ray that excuse didn't work for the Nazis and it won't work for you."

"NAZIs! What do the Nazis have to do with anything? I ain't no Nazi."

Tim just looked at the others, shook his head, and sighed.

Paige pulled Tim aside. "He obviously didn't do all this on his own. Someone had to tell him to do it. What are we going to do about that?"

"Let me think," he responded. "We've got him talking. I don't want to lose this advantage by moving him somewhere else. Let's question him more now, then figure out what's next.

"I think you've got him spooked somewhat. He thought you were dead, and now you've got him tied up. And you keep threatening him with bodily harm."

"Yeah, and I mean it, too."

"I think he can feel that. That's why I want you to question him. Find out who put him up to this if you can. Okay?"

Paige turned a five-gallon bucket upside down and sat on it, face-to-face with Billy Ray. She just sat there smiling an enigmatic smile at him while she twirled the stun gun in her hand. She slowly nodded her head.

For his part Billy Ray looked back at Paige, then around the shack — the others had gone back out — then back at Paige. He was sweating heavily, and kind of twitching while she remained calm and focused.

After a few minutes Paige sharply said, "Billy Ray!"

He jumped. "Yeah?"

"Billy Ray, you tried to kill me."

"No, I—"

"What do you think I ought to do with you?"

He glanced around as if hoping for someone to come and save him.

"No," she said, "there's no one here but you and me. What do you think I should do? Maybe I should return the favor? You think?"

He shook his head violently. "NO! You can't kill me. You're a good person. You'd never be able to do it. And they'd never let you get away with it. The law would find out and—"

"Maybe you're right," she said. "Hiding a dead body can be hard, can't it? Maybe I should just … tenderize you a little," and she snapped the stun gun toward him.

Billy Ray scrooched back until he was flat against the wall of the shack, his eyes goggling open.

"Maybe, if we talk some, I'll get to know you better," said Paige. "Maybe then I won't want to hurt you any more … in-spite-of-what-you-did-to-me."

Billy Ray looked like a bobble-head doll as he agreed.

"You from around here, Billy Ray?" she asked.

"Yeah, down to Simpkins."

"Simpkins? Like your last name." He nodded. "You one of the founding families?"

He nodded again. "My family's been there since forever."

"Bet they'd be right proud of what you done to me and that Dickson boy, huh?"

Billy Ray just sat there, head hanging down.

"Billy Ray, if you're from here we both know you weren't raised to hurt women."

He shook his head.

"So, why'd you do it?"

Billy Ray shook his head mournfully. "I didn't really want to. I ain't got nothin' against you. Didn't really have nothin' against that boy, neither. But when he told me to do it, that if I wanted to keep my job and help the others in the fleet keep theirs, I didn't see as I had much choice."

Paige nodded, urging him to continue his narrative.

"He said that Dickson boy was a reporter and that he had something on the big boss, and that if he got it in the paper, they'd stop the pogiefishin' in The Bay. That'd put me and a lot of other people on the beach. So I snatched the boy up, took him to the breakwater, and tied him up."

"And strangled him," Paige said.

"NO! Well, like I said before, not a purpose. He struggled and fell while I was getting him tied down. Guess he hit his throat then. He looked to be having some trouble breathing, but I couldn't worry about that. I just wanted to get him tied and get shut of there. Would've worked good, too, if'n you hadn't come along. No one knew he was missin', then when they found the skeleton didn't no one know who it was. But you had to keep pushing to find out who he was. Sheriff's people were satisfied to just call him a John Doe, but, no, you had to keep pushing."

"And that's why you tried to kill me?"

"I didn't think so much of it as tryin' to 'kill you.' I'se jest getting you outta the way. I was just gonna leave you there on the breakwater. I wan'tgonna kill you ... as such."

"Uh, huh." There was no way Paige was going to sympathize with this guy. He'd almost killed her. But she could grudgingly understand his twisted thinking. Leaving her for the elements to kill wasn't the same as him actively *killing* her. She shook her head. *Amazing what you can convince yourself of.*

"All right, Billy Ray, so who who told you to do that to Jon Dickson and to me?"

He shook his head disconsolately. "Cain't say."

"CAN'T SAY? WHY THE HELL NOT?" she yelled.

"It'd cost me my job if'n I told you."

Paige shook her head in wonder. "Billy Ray, you aren't going to have a job after this, don't you understand that? You've committed one murder and tried a second. They're not going to just slap you on the wrist and let you go back out into The Bay. You're heading for Nottaway Correctional in Burkeville. No pogiefishin' there. You get lucky they might teach you a trade making furniture. Of course, they only let around 80 inmates do that … out of the population of 1100. But, hey! You might luck out."

Now Billy Ray was looking purely mournful. It was at this point that Tim came back in .

"So, you ready for Nottaway?" he asked. "Or maybe we can get you into a federal lockup, like Supermax out in Colorado."

Billy Ray was trembling, now. "Come on," he almost whimpered, "can't you give me a break?"

"If you cooperate, they might take that into consideration," said Tim.

Totally defeated and deflated, Billy Ray said, "Whaddya want to know?"

Smiling, Tim asked, "Who told you to take the Dickson boy?"

Mumbling, he answered, "My captain."

"And who's that?"

"Kent Bulloch."

"And who does Mr. Bulloch get his orders from?"

"Damned if I know," grumped Billy Ray. "All's I know is that Captain Bulloch told me to get rid of the boy on the Kiptopeke Breakwater, and I did."

Paige asked, "And did he tell you to get rid of me, too?"

Subdued, Billy Ray just nodded his head.

"And you don't know who told him to do it?"

"No, sir."

Chapter Twenty-Nine

IT WAS TEMPTING to just leave Billy Ray tied up on the floor Nott's shack, but Tim's FBI training wouldn't allow that. Instead they took him to Eastville and borrowed a detention cell at the county jail to hold him. Then they all went out to Paige's apartment to strategize.

"Drinks?" asked Paige.

They all wanted beer so Paige pulled three bottles of Cape Charles Brewing's Puddle Pirate from her refrigerator.

As they sipped their brews in contemplation Paige asked, "What now? Do you go out and arrest Kent Bulloch?"

Tim shook his head. "No, that wouldn't achieve what we want. We want to know who at the top ordered all of this. Remember Billy Ray mentioned protecting 'the company.' I want to know how high up this goes."

Nott nodded. "From what the newspaper man Wayne Creed said, this might go all the way to Richmond."

They decided that the first thing they needed to do was to get someone into the company. Since they had Billy Ray in custody, but *incommunicado*, they'd have someone take his place when the taxi boat came to ferry the fishermen out to the factory boat. Being official and officious, Tim wanted it to be an FBI special agent. That would be safer also, he thought, than risking a civilian.

Paige argued that wouldn't work. "It would take you too long to get an undercover agent over here, and brief him on what is going on, and train him up to where he can pass for an Eastern Shore waterman."

Reluctantly Tim had to agree with her assessment. "Well who do we send, then?"

Paige turned and looked at Nott.

"Wha-what?" he stuttered. Nott's latent PTSD was starting to surface.

Soothingly, Paige said, "Nott, you're the closest thing to a full-fledged waterman that we have. And you know what all is going on. We'll dress you in your old clothes and boots and put Billy Ray's cap on your head and send you out to the boat."

"You don't really expect me to pass for Billy Ray, do you?"

Paige said, "No, of course not. But you can tell them you're his ... cousin, and that Billy Ray decided that bunker fishing was too hard for him. So he stayed ashore, and you went in his stead. They'll take you on instead of sailing short-handed. Hopefully."

Nott swallowed hard. "Hopefully?" he quavered? "And what happens if they don't?"

"How well can you tread water?" asked Tim with an amused grin. "No, if they don't accept you they'll probably just send you back in the taxi boat."

"Probably?"

"Yeah. Let's give it a try. Now, what do we hope to find out with Nott on the boat?" asked Paige.

"Well, I guess he needs to ask about the whereabouts of Jon Dickson," said Tim. "But he's going to have to be careful. Work for a couple of days getting the lay of the land before you begin asking any questions of your crewmates. You know? And try to avoid Bulloch as much as possible. He's been a captain for a long time and is probably pretty sharp evaluating his men. He's probably the one who sniffed out Dickson. Just be subtle. "

"S-s-subtle?" said Nott, his voice shaking.

"You can do it," said Paige. "I've got faith in you."

"Just don't push it," said Tim. "If you get any resistance, let it go. We don't want you getting hurt. These guys obviously are not afraid of violence."

"Oh, great," said Nott. "Do I get a gun?"

"Absolutely not," said Tim. "But we'll keep an eye on you. Don't worry, but be careful."

I don't know how they expect to keep an eye on me, Nott worried.

"We'll keep you in our prayers as well," assured Paige.

"Hmmph," snorted Nott. "Well, at least St. Peter will know who I am when I reach the pearly gates."

Chapter Thirty

AS THEY WAITED in the dark for the taxi deadrise to arrive, Paige was almost overwhelmed by the fragrance of a gardenia bush in someone's nearby yard. She fought to keep her concentration on the job-at-hand. They didn't want Nott standing out with the other men waiting to ferry out to the factory boat. Didn't want too many questions asked yet. They could see the men on the dock looking around for Billy Ray as they smoked and waited.

The rumbling sound of a diesel engine entering the harbor echoed over the water, the running lights of the deadrise glowing green-and-red as it eased into the dock. The waiting men continued to look around for Billy Ray and then climbed down into the boat. It was then that Nott emerged from the shadows and ran to the boat waving his hand over his head for them to wait.

"Who're you?" asked the boat driver.

"I'm Billy Ray's cousin, Claude."

"Where's Billy Ray?"

"He decided to stay on the beach. Said he was sick and tired of bunker boats and constantly smelling like fish. He's going to look to get a job driving truck on one of Nottingham's farms."

The other fishermen shook their heads. "Shite," said one of them. "Ain't gonna make nowhere near as much. Well, that's his concern. C'mon. Let's get out to the boat." And they motored off.

They got out to the mother boat. As they circled around her stern Nott noticed that her name was "EZKEEL." 'Strange name for a fishing boat' he thought to himself.

They pulled in to a boarding ladder and he followed the others aboard, keeping his cap low over his face. It wasn't like a military vessel, there was no one waiting to greet them, so he simply followed the others to the crew's quarters in the forecastle.

"Which bunk was Billy Ray's?" he asked.

"Over there," came the reply, and the one fisherman pointed to a squalid bunk with a locker next to it.

"This his gear?" asked Nott, getting a nod for a reply. Taking the moldy stained sea bag he found in the bottom of the locker, Nott emptied the gear. As he stuffed the belongings into the canvas sack he looked to see if there were any clues amidst Billy Ray's stuff. He found a piece of paper, crumpled up into a ball. He slipped it into his pocket. He'd wait until he was alone to look at it.

The rest of Billy Ray's belonging were just some smelly clothing and a working life vest, an orange hard hat, and a pair of heavy work gloves. These he put aside for his own use.

It was getting late. Work began at sunrise and continued to sunset, and the boat was moving toward the first catch site. The crew settled in their bunks and soon the snoring sounded like a diesel mechanic's shop. Glancing around Nott felt certain that he was not being watched. He pulled the blanket over his head, snapped on a tiny flashlight, and smoothed the crumpled paper note on the malodorous mattress. It was a note to the boat's captain:

Bulloch-

There's a spy in your crew, an investigative reporter. His name is Dickson. Find him and eliminate him. I don't care how. You'll be rewarded. Make sure you get rid of this note.

L.X.

Apparently, the captain had used the note to give his orders to Billy Ray, and Billy Ray's idea of disposing of the note was to just ball it up. This was proof for the murder of Jon Dickson being ordered by Kent Bulloch, but who was the "L.X." who signed the note? Maybe Tim would have an idea about that. Nott folded the note and put it in his wallet. It wouldn't do to lose this crucial piece of evidence. He rolled over and went to sleep.

It seemed like he had only been asleep for a few minutes when he was roused by the ringing of a brass bell mounted to the bulkhead by the hatch into the forecastle. He was already dressed, so he pulled on his white rubber boots, splashed some water in his face, and followed the others into the galley for breakfast.

This would be his first serious test. He knew that just showing up in Billy Ray's stead was going to be dicey, but he didn't know whether he'd pull it off or not.

"Who the f**k are you?" asked the cook as Nott shuffled up to get his breakfast.

"I'm Billy Ray's cousin," said Nott.

"Okay," answered the cook, "you're Billy Ray's cousin. But what the f**k are you doing here? And where's that peckerwood Billy Ray?"

Nott smiled. "He stayed on the beach. Said he was sick of smelling like a fish and he was going to go to work on a farm, or something."

"And he sent you instead?"

"Yeah, something like that."

"Does the company know that you've signed on?"

"Well," Nott said, "I'sehopin' to jest go to work and when they saw I could fill in good for Billy Ray they'd just hire me on in his place."

"The cap'n know about this?"

"Well, no," said Nott. "I'sekindahopin' to present it to him as already done once I helped get some fish on board. Figured if I done okay and we had a good haul, he'd be open to letting me stay."

Frowning, the cook walked away. He crossed over to a wall-mounted telephone. Nott figured he was calling the captain to inform him of this new situation. He was right.

The galley hatchway burst open and a red-faced bearded man came rushing in and right up to Nott, getting in his face. He towered over Nott and must have outweighed him by 100 pounds.

"Who the hell are you?" yelled Captain Bulloch. Nott could smell coffee and tobacco on Bulloch's breath and he jerked back from a fine mist of spittle. Bulloch was so incensed that he was almost foaming at his mouth.

"I'm here to work the nets," responded Nott.

"Who told you to get on my boat?"

"Well, my cousin, Billy Ray Simpkins. He decided he didn't want to fish any more. He told me and I thought maybe I could come out and take his place."

"You what?"

"I jest thought that I could take Billy Ray's place. One net-hauler should be the same as another, right? Ain't no big deal."

"Yeah it is a big deal," growled Bulloch. I don't take just any bum on my crew. I don't know who you are. I don't want a stranger on my boat. We got to work close together. We got to trust the guys working around us. I don't know you. I don't trust you. And I don't want you on my boat."

He turned to the mate standing next to him. "Mike, get on the horn and call the taxi boat to come out and get this guy. But first, secure him in the crew's quarters until we can off load him."

Nott protested, "Wait a minute! All I wanted to do was work on your boat." Actually, Nott was relieved. He'd been wondering if there was any way he could get off the fishing boat without having to pull nets for a week. He'd protested, but he was secretly relieved. Bulloch had killed one spy. This could have gotten messy.

It was several hours before the deadrise came out from Cape Charles to ferry Nott ashore. The situation was not good for Nott. He was scared and alone, and once again he started to lose contact with reality as his PTSD tried to spring forth. He spent the time just sitting on his bunk, forcing himself to think about Tim and Paige waiting for him on shore. Thinking. Worrying.

Chapter Thirty-one

WHEN THE DEADRISE dropped him off at the Cape Charles wharf Nott walked to the police department and borrowed their phone to call Tim's cell phone.

"I'm back," he said. "Can you pick me up at the Cape Charles PD?"

"You're back awful quickly," responded Tim. "They catch you?"

"No. The captain just didn't want a stranger on his boat."

"Did you learn anything?"

"I ... I'd rather not talk over the phone. Come and get me."

Tim had been at Paige's apartment on the beach in Eastville and it took him twenty minutes to get to Cape Charles. As soon as they were in Tim's car headed north Tim glanced over at Nott and asked, "Well? What'd you find out?"

"Wait until we're with Paige," Nott responded. "I still need to calm myself down."

When they got to the Wilkins Beach apartment, and each had a Cobb Island IPA in hand, Nott reached into his pocket and produced the soggy note. He handed it to Tim.

"What's this?" he asked.

"I found it in Billy Ray's traps. Thought you'd find it interesting."

Tim unfolded the note and read it. "Omigosh! The smoking gun! Look at this, Paige."

Paige read the note. "Whew! I guess we've got Captain Bulloch by the short and curlies. But who is 'L.X.' that wrote the note?"

Tim rested his elbows on his knees. "The company that runs the fishing fleet was sold about ten years ago. The corporate name is now Yúyóu PLC. Chinese. The CEO's name is Liam Xie , 'LX.' His office is in Norfolk."

"Well, let's go get him," she said.

鱼油

As they drove across the Chesapeake Bay Bridge-Tunnel Tim called his office and arranged for a warrant to search the offices of Liam Xie. He also arranged for an FBI task force to meet him there so that they could confiscate computers and files to further their investigation into the possibility of Yúyóu's lobbying efforts in Richmond skirting legality.

From the outside the offices were nondescript, sitting on the bank of the Elizabeth River in an industrial zone. Upon entering, however, they were overwhelmed by the opulence. Oriental tapestries draped the walls, delicate minimalist flower arrangements adorned the tables, and an armed guard, leather and buttons gleaming, stood at attention near the door.

The guard looked at them questioningly.

"Mr. Liam Xie, please," said Tim as he flashed his credentials.

Properly impressed by Tim's officiousness, and the fact that he had a complete FBI team with identifying jackets and badges, looked at him in consternation and stuttered out, "Mr. ... Mr. ... uhh ... he not here. He rushed out just about thirty-minutes ago."

"Where was he going?"

"He ... he said he had a flight to catch. He keeps a helicopter out to Norfolk International. He had me call and tell them to get it ready for a brief off-shore flight."

"Damn," said Tim, then looked at Paige and apologized. "Sorry." He looked at another Special Agent. "Go in there and seal everything up. Take anything that looks interesting—computers, files—you know the drill." The other man nodded. Tim glanced toward his car. "I'm going to the airport."

With blue lights flashing in his grill Tim raced to the FBO at the airport. Hurrying into the office he demanded of the surprised young girl, "Has Liam Xie taken off, yet?"

Startled she replied, "Yes. About fifteen minutes ago."

"Did he file a flight plan?"

"Well, his flight plan was kind of perfunctory. He said he was just going to fly around the mouth of The Bay to see if he could spot any fish schooling. That's all."

Cursing under his breath Tim went back to his car. Furiously he slammed the door behind him and said, "He's gone. Him and his helicopter."

"Can't you track him?" asked Paige.

"Sure. Come on," said Tim. "Have you ever been in the tower at an airport?"

They drove to the tower. Tim used his credentials to badge them in, and they entered a world of radios and radar screens and bustling activity.

"Who's in charge?" asked Tim.

"That'd be me," answered a pleasant-looking middle-aged black man. "What can I do for you?"

"Can you track the helicopter that took off from your FBO about twenty minutes ago?"

"Sure. Frank," he called, "have you got that chopper on your screen?"

"Yessir. It's about twenty miles past the sea buoy and just set down on the deck of a big ship out there.

ABOARD THE MASSIVE container ship, Zhoushan Island, in international waters and bound for its home port of Hong Kong, Liam Xie lit a cigarette while sitting in the luxurious owner's cabin. *It's not as nice as my office. Or my apart-*

ment. But it will have to do. *Really nice ceramics they've got here. Wonder what dynasty they're from.*

With both hands he smoothed back his shiny jet-black hair. *Too bad*, he thought, screwing a Dunhill cigarette into an onyx holder. *I was beginning to enjoy the decadence of Norfolk. Well, it was not my fault it all blew up. Maybe they'll find another nice rich assignment for me. But, please, no more fish!*

Epilogue

IT TOOK 32 days for the vessel Zhoushan Island to sail from Norfolk to its home port of Hong Kong by way of the Panama Canal. Xie thought of it as a relaxing cruise and spent much of the time sitting in a deck chair in the sun. He did lament the loss of his government-sponsored company in Norfolk, but knew that as far as seed money went, there was lots more where that had come from. He had done a good job with the menhaden business, and his superiors would welcome him back and have another opportunity for him to make them money.

The Zhoushan Island docked under the huge container-handling gantry cranes in Victoria Harbor, Hong Kong. Xie didn't watch the evolution. He was busy in his cabin preparing to disembark.

There was a quiet knock at his cabin door.

"Enter," he called.

The ship's first mate stuck his head in. "The gangway is out, comrade, and the pilot has already gone ashore."

Xie walked out the door. "Bring my valise," he ordered the mate.

At the head of the gangway, he looked down and saw a gleaming black Rolls-Royce Cullinan with blacked-out windows waiting for him. A back door was open and a liveried chauffeur stood waiting.

Ah, he thought. *Just as I deserve. All hail the conquering hero.*

He was climbing into the back of the car when he realized the interior was empty.. He started to climb back out asking, "Where—" when the chauffeur violently shoved him into the back seat, slamming the door.

"Wait a minute," cried out Xie. "Wait! What's happening?"

The driver threw his cap on the seat, started the car and drove quietly from the container yard. Xie was never seen again.

Back in Virginia the FBI waited until the FV EZKEEL docked with a hold full of menhaden. As soon as her lines were secure a team of agents swarmed aboard, guns drawn, and arrested Captain Bulloch. He was charged with murder and conspiracy to commit murder. Bulloch complained loudly that he had been set up. "I didn't have no choice. It was that little bas***d Xie. He swore that if I didn't do it, he'd make *me* disappear. What could I do? I hadda protect me and my family."

In Richmond, certain legislators lamented Xie's departure. The industry lobbyists assured them, however, that if they continued to support the menhaden industry, they would continue to reap the benefits thereof.

And on The Bay, the menhaden fleet kept sailing. The first mate quickly moved his gear into the cabin previously occupied by Captain Bulloch, and the FV EZKEEL only lost a half a day of production. The industry continued to lobby in Richmond for the legislature to ignore the Atlantic States Marine Fisheries Commission coastwide cap of 51,000 tons of fish and stuck with the state's 87,000 ton limit.

The pound fishermen continued to see fewer pogies end up in their nets, and the sport fishermen continued to worry about the reduced catches of rockfish, bluefish, and other game fish that would normally feed on the menhaden in the upper reaches of The Bay.

Nott was happily back in his oyster shack in Cherrystone Creek. Insistent Donna herself had purchased him a new iPhone and put the monthly bill on her own account. Maybe now she wouldn't have to roust poor Jim to run out in the creek looking for Nott when there was anything afoot. Nott gratefully acknowledged the gift, allowing her to demonstrate to him all of its bells-and-whistles. As soon as Donna's back was turned, Nott turned the phone off and slipped it into his pocket.

And Tim and Paige continued to walk the narrowing beach in Cape Charles, chatting and laughing and eating their brown dog ice cream cones before they melted and ran down their arms. They talked about how the winter storms were washing the beach away and how it would impact Cape Charles' newly-blossoming tourism industry. They shook their heads at the occasional bunker boat that seemed to be coming right up on the shore. They sat, hand-in-hand on the sandbar at Jackspots and watched the sun melt into the glorious Bay. And they studiously avoided talking about the future, afraid of jinxing what they already had together.

Preface

THE EASTERN SHORE of Virginia is a real place. A wonderful place. If you want to read some more about it try AN EASTERN SHORE SKETCHBOOK by David Thatcher Wilson.

Most of the names in the book are amalgamations of the names of people from the Eastern Shore of Virginia (ESVA). I felt that using Shore-common surnames like Kellam, Smith, Goffigon, Heath and others would add some verisimilitude to my story. They are not based on any real people, living or dead. Just borrowed the surnames.

Come visit our website:

Smith Beach Press

HTTP://SMITHBEACHPRESS.COM

From The Author

I WANT TO thank every one of you who take the time to read my books. You are the reason I keep writing, and I wish I could meet y'all in person. Maybe to share a café con leche at Cape Charles Coffee House.

Will y'all help me out? If you have enjoyed this book, please tell your friends about Paige. And if you really want to help out an independent author, post a short review on Amazon. Doesn't have to be fancy. Or even grammatical. Just let me know that you enjoyed the book. I promise I'll read each review. Word of mouth is an indie author's best friend and is much appreciated.

God Bless!
Emma

Acknowledgements

I NEED TO thank Don Rich (the COASTAL ADVENTURE series) one of my favorite authors, who convinced me to keep writing. David Thatcher Wilson whose Demon Series book THE EXQUISITE CORPSE gave me my main character, Paige Reese, fully developed.

Donna Bozza, mentioned in the book, is the Executive Director of the Citizens For A Better Eastern Shore, a group dedicated to saving the Eastern Shore from polluters, developers, and other n'er do wells. (http://www.cbes.org/index.html) Donna, I hope that you and Jim Baugh approve of how I included you in the book.

The Cape Charles Coffee House exists and is a delightful spot in downtown Cape Charles. They are in a beautifully restored bank building. You really should check out their website at https://www.capecharlescoffeehouse.com/. Also look into *brown dog ice cream*, http://http://www.browndogicecream.com/

On the highway across the street from the Barrier Island Center, is Machipongo Trading Company (http://www.esvamtc.

com/), another wonderful spot for coffee, sandwiches, soups, and sundries.

And as improbable as it sounds, Yuk Yuk and Joe's is a popular watering hole in Eastville. Looks like a dive from the outside, but inside you'll find warm Shore courtesy and great fresh seafood.

I'd also like to give credit to http://DonRichBooks.com and Florida Refugee Press, LLC of the Coastal Adventure Series of books for use of Mallard Cove Marina™, The Cove Beach Bar™, and The Cove Restaurant™.

I never was so devoted to reading a book's acknowledgments as since I became an independent author. Now I understand how important a section it is. Accordingly I would like to effusively thank my editor Debbie Maxwell Allen. I send her dreck, and through some sort of alchemy she returns to me polished prose. I don't know how you do it, but I praise you for it.

I want to also praise Shayne Rutherford of Wicked Good Book Covers. Shayne doesn't just artistically create a cover, she works hard to create a "look" for an author's work. That identifyability (my own word) is invaluable.

Colleen Sheehan of Ampersand Book Design makes sure that the interior, the layout and artwork and typesetting, are all perfect. I've done this myself on a couple of occasions. Believe me; Colleen does it so much better.

And one of the most overlooked yet important marketing tools – the back cover copy. Yes, I just wrote the entire book, but to summarize it in one or two paragraphs, succinctly and enticingly enough to urge someone to buy, is a special art unto itself. That's why I have turned to the incomparable Shelley Ring to handle this task for me. Shelley, you do it so well and so easily. Thank you.

Finally, I'd like to offer an apology to my Eastern Shore brethren. For the sake of the story I had to take the occasional license with some of the facts. You'll catch them, though anyone not familiar with The Shore shouldn't even notice.

More by
Smith Beach Press

BOOK ONE OF THE CHERRYSTONE CREEK SERIES IS AVAILABLE AT AMAZON:

Buy Now at tinyurl.com/yccwjkzf

LEARN MORE ABOUT PAIGE IN THE EXQUISITE CORPSE, AVAILABLE ON AMAZON.

tinyurl.com/y9uul6q9

Emma Jackson

LEARN MORE ABOUT THE EASTERN SHORE IN AN EASTERN SHORE SKETCHBOOK, AVAILABLE ON AMAZON.

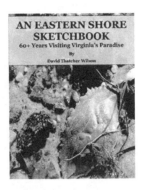

tinyurl.com/y77fxbcf

Free Book

WRITTEN BY MY MENTOR

dl.bookfunnel.com/oqf4nbi56e

SATAN. ACCORDING TO a 2007 Gallup Poll 70% of Americans believe that Satan, the Devil, is real. Another poll revealed that 42 percent believe people are occasionally possessed by the devil and a full majority, 51 percent, said people can be possessed by the devil or some other evil spirit. "Some other evil spirit." That's called "a demon." Do you wonder where demons come from? EZKEEL IN THE BEGINNING is the prequel to The Demon Series, but it is Biblically-based fiction that will answer that question for you.

Made in the USA
Las Vegas, NV
11 December 2023